MW01687953

HER LOVELY
LIES

ALSO BY K.L. CLARE

Lies That Bind Us

A Beautiful White Lies Novel

Her Lovely Lies

A Beautiful White Lies Novel

Vows That Bind Us

A Beautiful White Lies Short Story

February 2020

Lies That We Keep

A Beautiful White Lies Novel

Fall 2020

HER LOVELY LIES

A BEAUTIFUL WHITE LIES NOVEL

K.L. CLARE

WHITE ROSE PRESS

www.klclare.com

Published by White Rose Press

ISBN: 978-1-7329314-2-8

Editors: Katrina Diaz Arnold and Jaime Brockway

Cover design: © Sofie Hartley

Cover image: © Annie Ray, Passion Pages

Cover model: Caleb Johnson

For my sister, who introduced me to my first brotherhood.

But we loved with a love that was more than love—
Edgar Allan Poe

1

WILL, EIGHT MONTHS EARLIER

We watched her. We were too close. The rear studio entrance of the Stonington Fine Art Gallery was wide open, and I could not walk away.

The paintbrush in her hand swept over the canvas in a delicate rhythm, and the faint scent of lavender drifted into the alleyway. She was breathtaking as she sat before the easel and whispered the refrain of an old love song, the words floating from lush lips that I was desperate to taste.

Ellie James didn't know it yet, but she was mine. I would take her home with me when the time was right. I would claim every beautiful piece of her. And I would destroy anyone who stood in my way.

Sweat beaded on my forehead and ran down the sides of my face. While England's climate was generally humid, the late July heat in Connecticut was more so.

"You disregarded my advice and came for her anyway. You refuse to consider that you could be in love with the idea of her, not with the woman herself. Yet you've hesitated for weeks, brother. It's time to come home," Ethan said.

"Screw you and your psychoanalytic bullshit, Ethan," I said, bending to scratch the head of a thin retriever mix who had planted himself at my feet. "I'll approach when I believe she's ready. Why are you here? You had no role in that meeting yesterday. It was nothing more than a formality for me to counsel the transition team on the contract points of the New York acquisition."

"We're partners, remember? I'm flying back to London tomorrow night, anyway."

I jerked my head in a quick, slight movement to loosen a joint in my neck, then straightened and locked my stare onto Ellie again. Ethan and I had never shared meetings—we had shared a fondness for dividing and conquering—so something else was going on. "Do you have plans to see her sister before you leave?"

"It's quiet enough, and we can see they're safe, so there's no need. Our being here is creating unwanted notice, and I know you don't want that for her, Will. We can shut it down now if we all get on the plane tomorrow evening."

Ellie abruptly spun on her metal stool and stared in my direction as if she sensed my presence. I extended my arm and forced Ethan out of her line of vision but remained where she could see me. I wanted her to see me. I wanted her to feel me. Someone called out to her from the front of the gallery, and she startled, looking away before making eye contact with me.

"Christ, you know it's too late for that. Someone has been out there making noise for weeks. I don't know yet if it's meant to be a threat, but whatever it is or is not, I will end it."

"There's no proof of the Order's reformation. Our intel has always been reliable." Ethan palmed my shoulder. "God help whoever is troubling you," he added.

Ethan was careless when it came to our training. Our father never beat it into his character as he had with me. He'd understood early that my brother would always value a financial bottom line more than the pact that tied our family to Ellie's. Money drove Ethan and clouded his thoughts, influencing every decision he made, so our father had placed the burden of his legacy on my shoulders.

A few years after our father's death, Ethan and I earned millions through our private equity firm specializing in leveraged buyouts and expansion capital. It wasn't long before those millions became billions, but the money served only one real purpose for me. My financial influence provided an advantage in the war to keep Ellie and her sister safe.

History always repeated itself. Another extremist would incite the conflict once again. Ethan lived in denial, but I had planned for the day when assassins would regroup and come for them.

"You should leave tonight," I told Ethan. "Go back to the firm and source more US projects for me while I'm here. I'll keep Ben on standby so I can move quickly by helicopter between here and Manhattan. John will stay with me as well."

"You know, I think I'll do that. Time is money, and I'm not making anything by spending my time round here." Ethan took out his phone and searched his contacts. "Make your move soon and get home," he ordered over his shoulder as he walked away, the stray following close on his heels.

"Get that dog something to eat," I called after him.

I turned back to the art gallery's open door and watched Ellie reveal her painting to the woman who had joined her. Her fingertips followed the wet brushstrokes in demonstration, the movement of her wrist was graceful, and the smile on her lips suggested that she had a secret she would never share.

The sun would set within the hour, and she would soon walk home alone.

And I would follow.

Ellie's face and that secret thrill on her lips as she had admired her work the night before replayed in my mind, and even my punitive workout earlier that morning did nothing to suppress my desire to see it again. I dropped the towel I'd wrapped round my hips after showering and pulled on jeans and a T-shirt.

Wait until she's ready.

There had never been a time in my life when I hadn't taken whatever I wanted, the consequences be damned. It was a reflexive trait that wasn't easily curbed. On top of that, and quite like my father, I had always been impulsive and obsessive by nature.

But I had somehow found the discipline to wait Ellie out . . . to give her time to grow and thrive as an individual before allowing my obsession to consume all of her, though I could feel the elasticity of it contracting. My self-discipline had stretched to its limit.

I needed to see her. I would claim one touch, maybe one kiss, then continue protecting her from a distance.

Fucking liar. You'll take everything from her. Don't touch.

I shook my head, my deliberations vacillating between what I knew was the truth and what I wanted to do, and jogged out to my car. The town celebration had already started, and this fucking liar wasn't about to miss an opportunity to see her there.

It didn't take much time to catch up to her—there she was on the street just a few feet ahead of me. I would recognize her pretty arse anywhere. Stonington's main streets were narrow, so I retreated into the crowd and crossed to the opposing curb from where I could see her face.

Ellie soon found me and locked her eyes onto mine, and what I discovered in her gaze was staggering. It caused a sharp pain to cut through me as if a blade had pierced my heart.

Abandonment. Loss. She believed she was alone.

I pressed my palm against the center of my chest to ease the abrupt tightness.

Christ, how many times had she been failed?

She worked a second job tending bar for fuck's sake, and it

wasn't for the money—my father had assured me she had inherited her father's wealth, which meant she was looking for something or someone to make her feel safe and loved. She'd lost both parents at an early age, and her grandmother visibly held her affection for Ellie at arm's length. Ellie's sister, Isobel, seemed to express a maternal regard for her rather than offer the kind of companionship a sibling close in age could provide.

I had no idea how many men had passed through her life, but it was clear none understood who she was or what she needed because she was still alone.

She was practiced at concealing the pain, but beyond the beauty of her green irises, the suffering was there. I could see it and feel it, and in that moment, with our eyes locked, I knew that I would never find the strength to leave the States without her again.

Unrestrained thoughts raced through my head. I opened and closed my hands, flexing my fists as flashes of anger rushed through me. I wanted to kiss away the hurt. I ached to shelter her in my arms. I wanted to bury my cock deep inside of her and show her that she had been found. I lowered my eyes to her lips and smirked at the idea of her releasing all of that pain while screaming my name.

I met her eyes again, my smile fading as something more occurred to me. That she dared to hold my stare for so long revealed strength, but also there was something undeniable about the intensity of her will. Ellie held the power no one before her had ever possessed, and if I wasn't careful, one day she would wield it to put me on my goddamned knees.

Mine.

No.

I didn't deserve her. I would only cause her more pain. When she broke our connection to talk to her friend, I walked away.

2

WILL, NOW

Elle's kiss that morning was hot and cold, the intensity swinging between rushes of passion and indifference. She had been leaning against the white marble counter, scrolling through email messages on her smartphone, when I had pulled her out of the bathroom and into my arms.

She allowed her lips to fall away from mine and looked at the floor, her silence making me wonder which of my sins she had unearthed.

But the detachment in her kiss may have had nothing to do with me, and I hated that idea. I wanted everything about her to be about me—even if it hurt. Because if the fault was mine, I could correct my own missteps and make her happy again.

I pulled her chin up with my forefinger and forced her to reconnect. "Tell me what you need."

"Nothing. I'm fine . . . really." She forced a small smile to her mouth that didn't reach her eyes. "I just can't seem to push that dream from the other night out of my thoughts, you know?"

She called them dreams, but they were relentless fucking nightmares and one of the few things that I couldn't fix. I had taken the only action I could to help her. I'd hired a tenured professor from Cambridge who specialized in cognitive behavioral studies to counsel Elle in post-traumatic anxiety.

One exercise Elle embraced was writing to her dead sister about unresolved feelings. We'd created an email address for Isobel so that Elle could send messages and feel as if she were truly sharing private thoughts with her when she wanted to.

I released her chin and nodded. "I do know."

"You do, don't you?" she said softly, lifting her fingertips to my face. "We have so much to be thankful for, Will. So much opportunity before us."

"We do," I said. "How about dinner out tonight—just you and me?"

"We'll be mobbed—the press never misses our date nights—but yes, I'd like that. Let your assistant choose the place. Sean's recommendations are always spot-on." A genuine smile hit her lips, touching her cheeks and those eyes. "You have another busy day, I'm sure, so why don't I come to the office at seven?" She whispered her next words in a tease. "I'll be the girl in the red dress."

"Keep that up, and I'll skip my first meeting and tie you to the bed."

I hadn't ever done that—tie her up for sexual satisfaction. She submitted to me in a way that was perfect for us. Submission wasn't something she'd known before me, and she'd been rather inexperienced in bed on the whole—*thank Christ*—but she had caught on quickly and realized how well it eased us both. She had tenderly whispered more than once that giving herself over to me was like finding her way home.

Even so. I had drawn an important line that I would not cross with my angel.

I needed only for her to be submissive, not to be *a* submissive. Her sensual surrender was all it took for me to find a genuine sense of ecstasy—because she was the true source of my desire. From the moment I first touched her, sex became about loving her and feeling her rather than dominating her as it had been with women in the past. But in order for me to feel all of her and not miss the euphoric vibrations she was capable of sending deep into my soul, control and submission had to exist between us.

Possessing her body and soul when I was inside of her was that control.

"Hold that thought," she said. "I promise it'll be worth your wait. I don't want to be late for my first visit to the academies this morning, and I still need to get dressed."

Our first project as a couple after we returned from the US was the development of a charitable foundation. It was the perfect business venture in which Elle could get her feet wet, and my firm would benefit a great deal from the tax relief.

The mission for the Hastings Group Foundation was to provide disadvantaged and at-risk children a refuge in the arts, although the board smartly positioned the nonprofit for future expansion into other areas of support. We'd granted the Queen's request to announce our patronage to the public as the Earl and Countess of Sussex, a show of compliance to demonstrate our commitment to my pact with the Crown to let all things past pass.

"Making me wait again . . ." I gripped her arse and pulled her against my erection. "How's that working out for you these days, Wife?" I winked.

"I married you sooner than later because I love you madly, Will." She ran her hands up my jacket lapels and pushed her fingers into the back of my shirt collar, lifted onto her toes, and kissed my lips. "You waited for the dress as I asked, but making you wait any longer would have added nothing to who we'd already become."

Just as Elle finished her sentence, Joe Taylor knocked on our open bedroom door, signaling that he'd prepared the Bentley sedan I'd given her and that it was time to leave.

Taylor had been an infantry lieutenant for the Royal Army

before becoming the lead personal protection officer on the security team assigned to my wife's safety. Six former soldiers were on my payroll, two of whom had enlisted in the Met Police AFO ranks—authorized firearms officers—so they could legally carry a gun. I'd rendered the Order dormant once again by strategically releasing the details of the former leader Jack Lewis's death, but Elle's new title as a British countess and our financial status created additional security needs.

Elle and Taylor got on quite well. He had become like another brother to her, and I hoped like hell he never wanted to leave our service, because it would crush her.

As we had prepared for our marriage in the weeks before our late December wedding, she had asked me for one more thing apart from her original conditions: a solid commitment to family first. She longed for a large family, a family that was safe and secure and that she could fall into, with truths that she could never doubt. After Elle learned that Isobel hadn't been her biological sister, blood no longer defined family for her. She insisted we also choose family members based on love and loyalty, not only for the protection of our bloodline. And when Elle made a connection with someone, she anticipated the bond would last as long as she lived.

I directed a dismissive nod at Taylor and pushed a lock of hair behind her ear as he retreated downstairs.

Her head was small compared to mine, her face classically beautiful, and those green eyes of hers were mesmerizing. She rarely closed them when we kissed. Long layers of her chestnut brown hair painted with shades of blond fanned over the sleeve of my jacket, and her natural beach scent overwhelmed my senses. My blood vibrated, and the ever-present craving for her intensified. I needed her. I needed to absorb her into my soul to soothe the madness that lived in me.

I let my hand drop to her silk dressing gown and glide along the curves of her body, caressing the soft beauty I would never deserve. I had tried to walk away in the beginning, but in the end, I was too fucking weak to stay away and instead took everything from her.

I cursed beneath my breath.

"Don't," she whispered. "I know what you're doing."

I nodded and, shoving away the darkness of self-reproach, drew her bottom lip between both of mine. Her body responded to my tender kiss, and she melted into my arms the way she always did when we found the strength to let go of the past.

"You're amazing, Elle. I'll soon have everything in order so we can leave for Paris. I want you to understand that this travel isn't only about business—it's for us. This is time we need, time you deserve, so I'm making it happen for us."

She smiled again, and pure sunshine radiated from her. "That's beautiful, Will. I'm looking forward to it. Would you allow me to sit in on a few of the start-up meetings? Oh—and I would love to do some painting. I can't imagine a more inspiring place than Paris."

Thomas and I were moving forward with the expansion plan our brother had written before his death. Ethan and I had dreamed about it. We hadn't realized back then that our younger brother's mathematical genius was the key to getting it done. Thomas and I were in the process of settling details for formal operations in Paris, New York, and Madrid. Elle and I planned to travel to the European cities while Thomas would handle New York and the transition of current home operations into the London headquarters of our new, much larger organizational structure.

"Of course. You should come and go as you please," I said before pressing my lips to hers again. "I'll see that you have the materials to paint whenever you desire. And now . . . I must go to work before you think to remove this robe in my presence."

"Go then, savage," my wife told me as she twisted out of my arms and giggled.

I rushed down the staircase, gripping my side when a spasm reminded me of the gunshot wound that had caused permanent damage there. The bullet had annihilated the muscle mass as it passed through, and a secondary infection had set in. No matter how hard I pushed myself in the gym, that part of my body would never again be the same.

Taylor and three additional men were waiting in the foyer for Elle.

"No reporting back?" he asked.

I promised Elle freedom, and I needed her to know my word was good. I needed her to know she wasn't a prisoner in this marriage. I'd lose her if that were the case.

"It's not necessary, Taylor. Take two cars. Give her the autonomy to do as she chooses, but you do not leave her side for even a minute." I cuffed him on the shoulder on my way out the door. "She trusts you. Don't fuck that up," I added.

SHE BEGAN TO FLY

From: Ellie <ellie.hastings@hastingsgroup.co.uk>
To: Isobel <isobel.james@hastingsgroup.co.uk>

I'm compelled to touch my neck as I write this message to you. I drag my fingers along my throat and allow the tips to rest near my birthmark for a moment. Dreams continue to haunt me. *You* haunt me, Isobel.

Your image faded again briefly last night, but as you disappeared this time, I heard a faint rushing sound, like the fluttering of a butterfly's soft wings. I could see you again as you finally broke free from your chrysalis prison.

We were both free. You took flight, your new wings soaring gracefully, and my spirit drifted on a calm sea, bathing in its peace. I was wrapped in a blanket of light, free of fear and pain. I saw my father then. His smile was gentle and familiar, and his arms opened wide to receive me, but your watery image—your abruptly dark and expressionless face—appeared behind him. You were not love in this vision, though we had always loved each other. My father was not safe. I was not safe.

You both disappeared at once.

Another presence overwhelmed me, a soul extending itself, reaching out to anchor mine. I no longer wanted to be free—no longer wanted to drift through the sea alone. I opened my eyes, and Will's name touched my lips.

You see, Isobel, my mind paints you as a villain while I sleep, but in my waking hours, I won't allow my anger to take me there. You were protecting me. Even after all the lies, you were a good person—a good mother to Lissie.

I'm confused now more than ever, but I will find your truth.

3

Sean sat at his desk behind the glass wall that protected the audible privacy of the goings-on in my office. He handled sensitive matters for me, and I didn't want others at the firm listening in on his conversations.

Beyond his furniture and a quaint sitting area was more glass. Wall-to-ceiling windows faced south, with a view of the Tower Bridge that stretched from one side of the Thames to the other. Elle loved that view. She insisted that the sight of the bridge's Gothic towers combined with the sleek skyscrapers in the foreground drew the past into the present in the most beautiful way.

It was my wife's mind that was beautiful. Elle's conceptually driven brain showed her magnificence and purpose where I often saw disappointment and pain. She saw joy when I could see only gloom. Her mind and the way it worked was one of the most attractive things about her. It allowed her to easily accept and forgive, and that was a clear advantage for me because without it, she would never have been able to love a man like me.

"Good morning, sir," Sean said. "There are several urgent messages in your inbox. Never mind the unlabeled folder on your desktop. I'm uploading investor files into Thomas's new format, but it's not ready for your review. It's quite a lot of work to turn round, but once the tech changeover is complete, I agree it will be more efficient."

"Thanks," I mumbled, tugging at my collar.

"You're distracted. Is the countess all right?"

My executive assistant was one of the many people who had quickly embraced the use of Elle's title. For Sean, it was not only a term of respect but also of endearment. He was quite taken with her.

"Elle's fine. She'll pop in about seven this evening. You don't have to stay, but make dinner reservations for us. . . . You choose, she said. Move forward with extending that offer we discussed. I want her private secretary in place before we leave for the Continent."

He nodded. "I'll ask Ms. Smith to report to me until you indicate otherwise."

"Good. Train her to serve my wife well, Sean. Elle has no desire to spend much time here, so confirm with Ms. Smith that she agrees to work from Kensington when we're here in London. And run the NDA through my personal lawyers. Be sure the scope isn't so broad as to invalidate the agreement."

"Yes, sir. And I'll set up the library at Kensington myself."

Kensington was how we referred to our London home. It wasn't Eastridge, the majestic family estate Elle and I preferred, but it was elegant and comfortable and necessary. The three-story period house was located on the west side in an affluent neighborhood in the Royal Borough of Kensington and Chelsea.

No suitable houses for our unique security needs had been on the market when we looked, so I had financially coerced a film producer out of his home. I called in some favors from the sharks he had owed. The fucking wanker hadn't hired a lawyer, probably fearing he would wind up in court and that his standing in the entertainment industry would fall, nor had he understood that the gambling and drug-related debts I had settled on his behalf were less than the value of the property.

The day I had surprised Elle with the house, we had held hands as we passed through the gate into the front garden. She'd stepped up to the pair of glossy black doors and dragged her fingertips along the columns at the entrance while the nails of her other hand dug into mine. She'd said nothing at first. Anxiety pounded through her so forcefully that I could almost reach out and touch it, but once Mrs. Bates greeted us inside, Elle found the peace she needed to accept the house as our second home. She understood we weren't losing Eastridge.

It was Mrs. Bates who had then taken Elle's hand to parade her through the freshly renovated interior. Their relationship had come on fast and was important to both women. I could see how it filled another void for Elle. I had pretended to take an urgent call to give them some space.

When I had approached my mother and Mrs. Bates about staffing Kensington, both had urged me to provide Elle with the continuity of Mrs. Bates's presence in both houses. They hired a second housekeeper to oversee operations at Eastridge when Mrs. Bates was in London with Elle and me.

"Send roses," I snapped—at myself, not at Sean. "And send something to Lissie." We'd been away from our girl for too long. The adoption had been finalized on the same day Elle had married me. We were Lissie's parents by law, and we were growing to love her as if she were our own child. But it would take time before Lissie could think of us as more than Uncle Will and Aunt Ellie—and before Elle and I could think of ourselves that way too. We needed more time before becoming a nuclear family. After Lissie settled into the adoption, we would tell her that Ethan was her father.

I entered my office and closed the door after tasking Sean with finding Thomas, who was likely still sleeping in the penthouse above our offices after a night with another woman he'd never see again. Before I could sit and log onto the computer to retrieve my messages, the mobile phone in my desk drawer vibrated. I jerked open the drawer, tapped in the passcode, and read a coded text message.

I was about to receive validation for the knot twisting in the pit of my stomach.

A meeting with the director general of MI5—the National Security Service where my father had served as an intelligence agent before his death—had been secured as requested.

Good. They aren't screwing round with me.

ANGRY BROKEN HEARTS

From: Ellie <ellie.hastings@hastingsgroup.co.uk>
To: Isobel <isobel.james@hastingsgroup.co.uk>

You lied . . . and then you left me alone to live with those lies. God, you left me alone to raise Lissie.

Here's something I know you thought you'd never hear from me: I'm seeing a therapist, something you had pushed me to do after discovering my anxiety. I'm not sure it would have made a difference then any more than it does now. I'm doing it for Will, to make him more comfortable. He has sacrificed so much, given so much of himself to save me—so I will give him this.

I'm angry with you, Isobel. You were all we had, Lissie and me. We trusted you . . . depended on you . . . loved you. I hate that you and I never said those words. I hate that I loved you without owning it before I lost you.

I'm learning to open my heart, learning how to be less selfish. I hope so, anyway.

Lissie was the first to hear me say those three words. I smile now thinking of it, wondering if you are proud of me. It happened the day after we lost you. Even as she cried out for you, her little heart torn to bits, I knew she was part of me. Of course I thought she was my niece that day, with the same blood as mine in her veins. But there was something else. Something telling me that my connection to her wasn't just a predetermined biological link, that there was more to our story.

This morning, after Will left for work, I pulled out that report again—the one with the paternity results from the test Ethan had initiated before his death.

He's dead, too, but you know that. Another life lost because of mine. I sometimes wonder if he's there with you now. Are the two of you finally free to be together?

I'm staring at the photo of you and Ethan. I can see a mutual understanding between your heart and his. I don't know your story, but I want to know. I met Ethan, and in the short time we had together, he showed me the depth of his generosity and a remarkable love for his family. He'd said that he loved you. Did you and he experience the same kind of love that exists for Will and me?

Will and I are married now. I love him more than I can say, but I'm scared, Isobel, and you aren't here for me, to calm me, to mother me in your hot-tempered way. He continues to conceal the grief that remains after the loss of his brother, continues to hide the guilt he feels because Ethan isn't here for his daughter.

I know grief doesn't end and that it's the price for loving someone, but it should change—and Will's doesn't seem to be changing.

Ethan would have been a good father, and Lissie needed him. You took that from her. But there's something else you kept from your daughter. You were never truly my sister.

And you are not her mother.

4

Three hours later, I pulled up to the meeting place and cut the ignition only to sit quietly in my car, eyes forward, avoiding the sight of the dilapidated warehouse. I knew in my gut what I was about to hear from the director general, and I didn't have the strength to face it. It would hurt her.

Elle.

She would give me the strength.

"Call my wife," I told my phone's voice-command function after powering the phone back on. Hearing her voice right then was worth the risk of being located.

She picked up on the first ring, and her mood was much brighter than it had been that morning.

"Hi, handsome."

Her name was all that I could manage in response.

"Will, what is it? What's wrong?"

Pull your shit together. Don't upset her.

I cleared my throat and roused a smile so she could hear it in my tone. "Nothing's wrong. I just wanted to hear your voice before my next meeting. I may not have another chance before I see you tonight. How were the academy visits?"

I could see it well without even having to ask. The school children would be delighted to meet her. She had a natural allure that drew kids to her. They were comfortable touching her, clinging to her waist, or holding her hand, even if her attention was directed elsewhere. I'd watched her interact with her art students in the States, and it was something more than lovely to see.

Even Lissie's affection for Elle was breathtaking, growing into something that was yet to be defined but so fierce it nearly displaced the loss of Isobel.

Our conversation from weeks ago came back to me. We'd both been surprised by Elle's evolving maternal instinct—and my desire to support it, albeit reluctantly. She wanted us to have children of our own. It would be difficult for me to share her attention, to give up the pieces of her that they would take, but the truth was that I wanted our children as much as she did. Just not yet.

At least three, Will, she had said as we lay in bed after making love on our wedding night. Her thoughts had spilled out randomly. *Maybe more, if I can manage it physically. You and me . . . it's on us to grow this family. You know what it means to me to have a big family after not having one, or not much of one, in any case, and I know how important building a legacy different than your father's is to you.*

The exhilaration in her voice pulled me back into the present.

" . . . and the kids were great. The head teachers were really receptive. I think we can get into these schools sooner than expected. I'm excited for the board to reconnect with the Department for Education to identify the children who most need the program."

"Do it, Elle. Whatever you need. You have all of my resources at your disposal."

"I know, and thank you. I think it will help me as much as it will help the kids, will give me focus. Are you going to be late for your meeting? We can talk more tonight."

"Yeah. I'll see you tonight. No words, baby."

"No words," she repeated before we disconnected. It was our *I love you* but more. Three common words would never be enough. No words existed to express what we shared.

I turned off the phone once more, stepped out of my car, and headed for the warehouse, where a familiar face greeted me inside.

Director General Randall Martin drew me into his embrace. "Son, it's been a long time. I'm so sorry about Ethan."

"Thank you," I said, pulling back. "I'm sorry for the loss of your wife as well. Mother still talks so fondly about their years together."

"Ah, the lovely Mary Hastings. You're taking good care of her?"

"Yes, sir—"

"Let's get down to it, shall we? We don't have much time before one or both of us is located. You took out one of my agents several months ago, and I want to know why."

"The Crown commanded it. He was leaking information."

Martin's face grew inflamed with fury. "And what personal advantage did you gain for safeguarding the Crown's goddamned indiscretions?"

Anger rushed through my own blood. He knew why I had complied with the command—to protect Elle and avenge Ethan. "You know the answer to that. There is nothing I won't do to keep her alive. *Nothing.* You know this. You are aware of all that I've done."

He hesitated for a moment before nodding. "Yes, I've followed the situation. You're quite good at what you do. Quite the mercenary when the reward is great enough to please you. You are your father's son, a man of his making—forever his soldier of fortune."

I released the tautness in my neck with a slight jerk and flexed my fists to loosen them. There was nothing for me to prove to this man. He wasn't the enemy—his hard-hitting words were meant to examine my fortitude and evaluate my strength. He was forcing me to earn his trust.

Fucking intelligence agents.

"You know why I'm here, Director. Do you agree to provide the intel I'm seeking, or shall I find another source?"

Martin smiled. I'd passed his test. "I loved your father as if he were my own brother, you know."

I nodded. "Even when you couldn't rein him in."

"Indeed, even when I couldn't rein him in. You're right to be concerned, William. What you've done by marrying the James girl . . . well, you should have known what would come of it."

My gut clenched, and I looked to the crumbling cement floor. "I did know."

Marrying Elle created the assumption that we'd have children. Combining my blood with hers made the old line stronger, no matter that her patrilineal bloodline ended with her.

He reached out and gripped my shoulder with kind regard. "I see."

The silence between us echoed round the warehouse. It vaulted through rusting metal rafters, disturbed only by the tinny thumping from loose-hanging ventilation ducts.

"You can't give her children, son," Martin finally said. "Another extremist is out there lying in wait. He doesn't care that her claim was formally ceded. He will find followers, and assassins will come for her, come for your children."

The Order generally wasn't a family tradition passed down from generation to generation. Once it was eradicated, it ceased to exist—until new extremists found the cause to be relevant.

"Join my team, and I'll help you find him," he added.

WONDERFUL LIAR

From: Ellie <ellie.hastings@hastingsgroup.co.uk>
To: Isobel <isobel.james@hastingsgroup.co.uk>

My thoughts are random and unkind today. Dr. Clarke reminds me that this is a symptom of post-traumatic anxiety, though the severity of it is a slight regression for me at this point.

This afternoon she asked me to consider the similarities and distinctions between the two people I have loved most. The resemblances are few, but the difference is remarkable. You are a fraud, and Will is the only person who has been honest with me.

Dr. Clarke believes this perception is temporary and urges me to write more often.

I will try.

Do you remember our promise to Gran? We promised her that, at some point in our adult lives, we would help at least one person in need. More, if possible. You were twenty when we made that pledge, and I was seventeen. We took our oath seriously and decided to start right away by donating blood together.

I was wooed by the Red Cross because I'm a highly desirable

universal donor with O-negative blood, but you were not invited as frequently. You had a rare blood type: AB-negative.

Blood never lies.

I overlooked something the day Mary gave me the yellow envelope containing Lissie's paternity results. My mind was focused on confirming that Ethan was Lissie's father. I rushed to the end of the report, to the summary that supported the paternal match.

In my haste to confirm the DNA match between Ethan and Lissie, I neglected to review the other documents inside the envelope—until Will's lawyers requested that I locate it and send it to them to complete our adoption filings with the court.

Another report was in the envelope, and I'm holding it right now.

I don't know who she is, the woman with the O- blood type shown as the maternal match on the second report, but I intend to find out.

We both know it's not you, Isobel.

No one else could have known but me.

What a wonderful liar you've been.

5

Thomas was seated at the bar in my office with a mug of coffee when I returned to the firm. He was staring at the painting Elle had given me for my thirty-third birthday.

She had painted a memory that she'd said was burned into her mind and needed to be set free. It was a memory of Ethan, Thomas, and me . . . on the night Ethan was killed. The three of us were in the corridor of the hotel where we'd all been staying, our backs to her as we moved towards the exit. It was the night we'd hit the streets to go after the Order. They had come for her, had attacked the hotel with explosives.

I remember looking back at Elle one last time. I remember the horror in her eyes, though she had tried to hide it from me. I remember how desperately I wanted her to love me. And, in the very same space of time, I remember feeling the love I had for my three brothers. I had been in between Ethan and Thomas, shoulder to shoulder with them as we walked away from her . . . and that was the moment she had captured and painted for me. A moment when Ethan had still been by my side.

That stunning, heartrending work of art was the finest gift I had ever received. It held more meaning for me than one could ever know. But Elle knew—she'd taken every bit of emotion she could wring from me and released it onto that canvas. Once upon a time, everything in my life had had a price. But not now. Not her, and not that oil painting.

Thomas set his mug on the bar and stood. "Christ, I've been waiting here for over an hour. Sean said you went dark this morning. I know you weren't with Ellie because she—"

"Keep your reconnaissance to yourself unless she's in trouble. You know I promised to respect her independence, and if there's no danger, I'm not going to break my vow."

Elle searched for information about Isobel, and I had asked my brother to keep tabs on the situation in my stead.

"Yeah. There's no need to at this point," he said.

"Before we get on with other matters, I'll say that Elle wants everyone home for the weekend. John's taking the train from Loughborough tomorrow. He'll hit London round noon."

I had made a promise to my family after Ethan's death—more choices, less coercion. John's passion was football, and he was good, so we agreed to explore it for the remainder of his gap year. Loughborough University offered the best program in the country. I arranged for a midyear admission so John could settle into the athletic program and be prepared to hit the ground running at the start of his first official academic year.

Thomas nodded. "I have a meeting tomorrow evening—real-estate pitches for New York—but I'll get him from the station and drive home in the afternoon. It'll be easy enough to video conference into the meeting later. So, where the fuck have you been?"

"I went to see one of Father's old friends." I tossed an envelope onto the bar. "Eyes only," I added. "We'll discuss it this weekend. Right now, I want to talk about you cleaning up your fucking act straightaway, brother. I don't want the reputation of my company stained by your whoring, as it was by Ethan's."

I promised less strong-arming, not that I wouldn't be tough to some degree. Ethan and I had both stained the firm's reputation, each in our different capacities. Our current clients showed little concern for our past behaviors because they were making a lot of money. But the goal was to open up stakes and grow our catalogue of investors, so we needed to clean up for prospective backers who might perceive this kind of shit as a distraction.

Thomas pushed a hand through his hair and dug his fingers into his scalp as he examined the contents of the envelope. "Christ. *Jesus Christ*. Why didn't you come to me with this sooner? You know I'm here for you. We can't allow—"

"I want a commitment now, Thomas," I said to shut him down. Eastridge was secure, but though I owned the building, I couldn't be certain about the integrity of the offices or the Kensington house, for that matter. We couldn't control the countless variables of London's environment or its people in the same way we could with my country estate.

"Yes, you have it. You have my word." And his word was good because he was my brother, but resentment and condemnation showed in his eyes.

"Goddammit, Thomas. I'm not telling you to quit sleeping with women altogether. But you must be more discreet. As for the other matter, I do know you would never abandon me. Can you provide me with reassurance that Elle's project isn't relevant to the contents in that envelope?"

"Ellie's only seeking information about her sister. Are we still in agreement that there's no harm in her searching for that closure?"

"I sure as fuck hope that's still the case," I said.

6

I was standing before the glass wall in my office when Elle arrived. I nearly dropped the whisky from my hand as she entered the room. She was covered in an elegant black coat, but the shape of her curves teased what was hidden beneath the tailored cashmere. On most occasions I would have gone to her—hell, I'd crawl on my hands and knees to get to her if that's what she wanted—just not this time. This time I wanted to get lost in the sway of her hips. I wanted to take in every fine detail of my wife as she advanced towards me.

Her beauty never escaped me, never dulled, never grew ordinary.

"So . . . the tale is true. The powerful man in the tower is also the most handsome in the land," she said, her husky bedroom tone washing over me, promising that her thoughts were in the same place as mine.

"Don't romanticize my character, baby. It will only lead to disappointment," I countered.

"That's crazy, Will. There isn't a thing about you that disappoints."

I could no longer restrain my ego—it grabbed hold, and my

lips pulled into a tight smirk. Nothing pleased me more than knowing she wanted me. I drew her into my arms and pushed my growing arousal against her stomach. "Take off the coat. Show me what is mine."

Elle stared up into my eyes from beneath her lashes. "I lied to you," she said, dragging her fingers along the button placket on my shirt. "There isn't a stitch of red on my body."

"No? Well then, this may be the time I do smack that pretty arse of yours."

She sucked in a quick, sharp breath and moaned on the exhale. Her lids dropped, and her cheeks flushed with heat as if she'd just had an orgasm. I knew that look, knew my wife—she wanted me to do it.

Do not cross the line you've drawn for her.

"Or maybe this is just another one of your empty threats. Either way, you should probably lock the door." She stepped backwards out of my arms and unbelted her long coat, letting it fall to the floor at her feet.

Fucking. Christ.

I wanted nothing more in that moment than to feel her soul breach mine and heal me. I needed to bury my cock deep inside the beauty before me to find myself again—the real me, not the dark pretender who destroyed everything. That man, the one who was good and moral, lived only in her.

"It locked behind you. . . . Lift the dress."

Elle obeyed, slowly raising the skirt of her silk dress to reveal delicate knickers with little more than a lace triangle in the front and a matching garter belt. Similar lace at the top of her stockings peeked from beneath the thigh-high fuck me boots she wore. Every thread on her body was coordinated in the same nude color that blended well with her blushing skin tone.

I stepped closer, grabbed her hips, and pulled her against me, and the line I swore never to cross began to blur. I snarled in her ear, "What are you asking me for, Elle?"

She wrapped her arms tightly round my neck and dropped her face into my open shirt collar. "Make me feel *more*," she breathed onto my skin. She then lifted her head and locked her eyes into mine. "I'm not made of glass. You will not break me."

I bowed my head. It was merely a quick drop of the chin, but she understood it was more than a slight gesture. It was my vow to deny her nothing. Unanswered questions about the past cultivated a restlessness in her that scared me. I had lived too many years without her, and I would do anything to keep her.

Before I could reprogram my thoughts, I filled one hand with her arse and the other with a fistful of her hair, and I used both to pull her to my mouth. She strengthened the hold round my neck with her arms and slid her hands up the back of my head to press our mouths together harder, opening wide for my kiss. Her sweet taste hit my tongue, flooded my senses, and my desperate desire to control everything about this woman grew stronger and consumed me.

Elle dug her nails into the back of my neck and writhed against my cock. She knew what she was doing—she knew she was choosing to push me beyond that line.

"Give me more . . . " she pleaded.

I dragged my lips from her mouth to her ear and whispered, "For lying to me." And then I drew back my arm and allowed my hand to connect with a harsh smack against her bare arse cheek. I pressed it there to ease the sting.

A small cry escaped her, but she didn't move away from my hand. She pushed into it.

I drew back and landed another smack in the same place, but instead of easing the sting, I shoved her underwear away and slid my fingers inside of her. "For pushing me when you should not," I said against her lips after swallowing her erotic little cry.

She relaxed her grip on my neck, allowing one hand to fall to my chest, and hit me with her stunning eyes—eyes filled with an unexpected mess of lust and adoration . . . and victory. Her lips parted as she settled on my other arm and let her head fall back.

I've never seen anything more beautiful.

I need her.

She was my savior—that she loved me was the only thing that mattered, and hers was the only saving grace I would ever receive in this lifetime. I drew her mouth to mine and kissed her again when her orgasm clenched onto my fingers and her breath carried my name. With a quick snap of my wrist, I ripped apart her lace waistband.

"You're still taking the pills, Elle?"

"Yes, of course," she said with a playful smile as she freed me from my trousers.

That smile, the innocence of it mocked by mischief. And just like that smile, quite a lot about Elle was a series of contrasts—her pure, endearing traits were often baited with the promise of something wicked, and I couldn't get enough of it. It drove me mad. I was completely mad for her.

I lifted her into my arms, then put out one hand to steady my weight against the wall. I covered her mouth with mine and thrust into my angel much harder than I should have, and those fucking demons—the faces, voices, my father's fists—fled from my soul once again.

LITTLE GIRLS AND BOYS

From: Ellie <ellie.hastings@hastingsgroup.co.uk>
To: Isobel <isobel.james@hastingsgroup.co.uk>

I'm sitting in the car waiting for Will. He stands just outside my door in the brisk night air, finishing one last business call for the evening.

I wish you were here, Isobel. I'm tired of feeling subjugated by my childish fears. And the anger. I've been so angry, but tonight? Tonight I wish we could sit on your bed with a plate of Gran's soft cinnamon biscuits like we did as girls so that I could tell you about him.

We talked a lot about boys when we were growing up. It was one of the few areas of common ground we shared as sisters. Even as adults, we carried on with that one little thrill: the secretive midnight boy talks. It was similar to the tea parties we'd had in Gran's secret room as young girls, during which we had giggled about the silliness of the boys in our classrooms. But as we matured, the content of our chats did as well. The boys became men.

If you were here, I could tell you about Will. And between

biscuit munching, I would describe the boring stuff that makes me happy, like the first time I visited his office. . . .

As I was led through a second reception area, a large silhouetted figure moved toward me from out of the daylight cast through a wall of glass. The movement was familiar. It was confident, dangerous, carnal. It was Will's strut. As he came closer, the features of his handsome face were revealed.

Will's dark charisma never fails to captivate me.

He wore black that day, dressed in a suit tailored for his body. Despite his muscular build, his frame appeared tall and lithe. I remember how long and elegant his neck seemed and how the pale blue tie there complemented his beautiful eyes. Blue eyes that sparked with white fire. He stole my heart all over again.

His warm smile twisted into a panty-melting smirk, and he pulled me into his arms to kiss me. "I've missed you," he said, his deep voice low and full of gravel. He then led me to the wall of glass and showed me his incredible view of the River Thames.

I was floating euphorically. And then my lying brain told me I'd lost control of my body, that I was about to plunge fifty stories to my death. As my stomach tightened and trembled, he sensed my disorientation, wrapped his arms tightly around me from behind, and pulled me away from the wall, rescuing me from my own illusion.

Will knows what I need often before I do. He knows me beyond words. I'm not angry tonight, and it's because of him. And I need you to know this, Isobel. I want you to know that Lissie and me . . . well, we're okay without you. Because of him.

7

I kissed Elle's warm lips after climbing into the back of the Bentley with her. "That was David Nielson. He and Caroline are at the same restaurant and invited us to join them. It's up to you, baby. We can keep our private table if you fancy it."

"Do you need time to talk shop with David? I don't mind. I haven't seen Caroline since the wedding. I do like her, you know. I just prefer to take her in small doses."

"All right, we'll join them, but let's not make an entire night of it. And since we're no longer dining alone . . . close your eyes for me before we arrive." I winked.

Tiffany's was just a few blocks from my building, and the bright artwork displayed outside the storefront had grabbed my attention when I had been on the way to my meeting with Director Martin.

And here's an opulent interpretation of the key pendant. These stones are nearly flawless and colorless. This design is chic but quite sophisticated about it, the jeweler had explained as she presented me with a necklace.

Very much like my wife. I'm pressed for time—send the packaging and documentation to my office, I'd said as I had chucked my credit card onto the glass counter and had slipped the pendant into my pocket.

Elle closed her eyes, and I fastened the clasp at the back of her neck and kissed her throat above where the platinum and diamond key lay against her skin. Her pulse quivered against my lips. She held her eyes shut tight, touched the key for a moment, then reached for my face and rested her fingertips on my cheek.

"Your key," she whispered, and when she finally opened her eyes and looked into mine, I had no doubt those two small words combined had a profound meaning for her, for us. She got that I'd given her all of myself, and it made no difference to me what she called it.

It didn't matter how much or how little the cost—she marked every one of my gifts with a meaningful moment that we'd created together. I had come to depend on that, and it was the reason I needed to buy her so many things. She showed me how to combat the fear we shared—the fear of losing time—by collecting significant moments, memorializing them with these tangible objects, and treasuring them like precious jewels.

As we arrived in front of the trendy French restaurant where Sean had sent us, Elle kissed me softly on the mouth and told me that my key would always be safe with her.

"Let's go home to Eastridge tonight," I said, ignoring that the car door had been opened for our exit. I moved my lips close to her ear. "I don't want to wait until morning. I want to hold you in the bed where we made love on the night you became mine. And in the morning, we can surprise Lissie and take her to school."

Elle leaned in closer. Paparazzi cameras flashed. Neither of us cared right then.

London's photojournalists had come to realize it was easier to get what they wanted when they respected the boundaries I'd given them, so it was rare that one would do much more than take a few snaps before quietly moving on. It was safer for Elle—and much cheaper for me—if we allowed them to get a quick photo when they found us out for dinner or social events. City pavements were fair game, but anything else was off limits.

"I belonged to you before we were married, Will. But I want that too. Take me home. I want us to be home with our family."

Colin Wilson, who was one of the personal protection officers on my security team and our driver for the evening, cleared his throat. "Sir," he said. "More cameras are headed this way. Evans will assist you with cover while I drive over to the car park."

Whenever Elle was out on her own, she was accompanied by at least four men, but when we were together, we usually had only one or two with us. No one would get through me—I would take another bullet for her without question—but my wife was becoming quite good at pushing the boundaries of our protection agreement, so more eyes were better.

I ducked out of the car and helped Elle get to her feet, and we did our thing. Behind me, she straightened her dress and popped into the pretty pose her stylist had showed her. "Like a teapot," she liked to tease. I moved aside and placed my hand on the small of her back, and we both smiled for several seconds for the cameras.

"That's it, everyone. Good night," I told the gaggle of photographers as I tucked Elle beneath my arm. Andrew Evans moved into position on her left.

David waited inside the entrance and led us to the table, where Caroline rose from her chair with her arms held open wide. "Ellie, darling, I'm so happy you're joining us. It's been too long since we've had a chat," Caroline said as she embraced Elle with genuine warmth.

"I can't wait to catch up," Elle said, then redirected her smile to David when he took her hand to welcome her as well.

He did what most men do when they meet my wife's eyes for the first time or, in David's case, for the first time after a significant period had passed. He stood there entranced for a minute and then abruptly dropped his eyes, without doubt hoping like hell that I hadn't noticed his hesitation to look away.

Of course I noticed. I was the most jealous motherfucker to walk the earth when it came to her, and there would never be a time when I overlooked the reactions of others when they were near my wife.

My onetime roommate from Oxford University fumbled with his wife's chair, and I grinned like some cardsharp who had just won another hand.

But there was more to my awareness than ego. My father had trained me to consider every contact a threat and assess the significance only after securing the safety of my asset. There had only ever been one asset for me, and he had raised me to shield her from harm at all costs. And now that I loved her with a madness that couldn't be explained, the protective instinct was sewn so deeply into my fabric that it would always remain at the ready.

Waitstaff approached our table, each of the three displaying a different bottle of wine for our selection. A fourth waiter arrived holding a bottle of Elle's favorite Dom Pérignon vintage, and I nodded at that one. Sean knew his shit.

"Give the bottle to me before you open it here at the table." It had become habitual for me to monitor the source of Elle's alcohol. Thomas and I suspected that her wine had been drugged at a charity event not long ago. She'd had only a few ounces when her speech had slurred, and she'd complained of an unusual weakness in her limbs.

"Yes, monsieur, certainly. Chef requests the honor to greet the countess, if you please?"

Elle was already deep into conversation with Caroline. I caught her attention, knowing she would scold me later for my behavior if I denied the request. I smiled at her, thrilled by the thought of doing something more in the same evening to make her happy.

"Tell your chef we'll be happy to receive him," I told the waiter.

She rewarded me by placing her hand on my thigh beneath the table and squeezing.

"And please bring us a bottle of Glenlivet as well . . . 18 if you have it," David added.

After drinks were served and the chef visited our table with his recommendations, David and I waded into the details of some pending business transactions for a project we were undertaking through my firm. All the while, I couldn't help but notice the intensity of Elle's conversation with Caroline.

"So you're saying Commissioner Brown is your brother?" I heard her ask.

"Yes, he's my twin," Caroline confirmed.

"Join me in the ladies' room, Caroline," my wife demanded, pushing backwards against her heavy dining chair until I got to my feet and pulled it out for her.

ONLY WORDS BLEED

From: Ellie <ellie.hastings@hastingsgroup.co.uk>
To: Isobel <isobel.james@hastingsgroup.co.uk>

Will and I are on our way home to Eastridge for the weekend, and I am so relieved. I won't have much time or privacy over the next few days, so I need to get this out of my head now. I need to ask you something, Isobel. I need you to lead me to the answer.

The idea of finding the answer terrifies me. I'm afraid that one more truth could hurt us beyond recovery. And deep down, I know this one is meant for Will.

I've been carrying one of your photos around in my bag. You know the one—the photo of you and Ethan with Simon Parker.

God, he was your murderer, Isobel, the cruel man who shot you through the heart.

I promise you that he received the same death he gave you and Gran.

But what is the meaning behind this photo, and what will it do to us?

We know Ethan lied.

You lied.

Fear stirs in my gut now, and it tells me there is something more to the lies you and he shared, the lies that nearly destroyed us all.

The thought of discovering more betrayal unnerves me. And the thought of what it would do to Will if he were to learn that his brother lied to him further sickens me. He doesn't know this photo exists.

I can't see him hurt again.

I sent a copy of the photo with Caroline Brown Nielson tonight, and she has promised to deliver it to her brother, the commissioner for the Metropolitan Police Service.

Commissioner Brown interviewed me after your death to satisfy US authorities, and I knew the moment he entered the room that day that he was someone who would be kind, a compassionate soul who would help me.

I pray the commissioner agrees to assist me now in getting to the bottom of this photo. Not only does he have the necessary resources, but also he knew Ethan. I'm quite sure of that.

8

The kitchen was bustling with activity when Elle and I entered from the great hall after arriving late the night before. Mrs. Bates's brother had driven her back to Eastridge the evening before, and she had happily reinstated herself at the center of the commercial range, where she now fried eggs, back bacon, mushrooms, and sausages.

Elle peered over Mrs. Bates's shoulder, placing her hand there for a moment—something the rest of us would never dare to attempt. "The bacon smells wonderful. Can I help with anything?"

"Not in this house, you know. Your toast and jam are on the table with the coffee. Go on, then. Mary and the children will be down any minute." Mrs. Bates patted Elle's hand and gestured to the opposite end of the enormous kitchen with her chin. "The lads were made to wait as you asked, William. Everyone eats together this morning," she added.

"Won't you leave the rest of the cooking to your staff and join us, Ina?" My mother approached from behind and opened her arms wide for Elle. "Ellie, dear, come here. I have missed your company." Mother pulled back from their embrace and surveyed us both. "The two of you look quite well. How much time do I get with my daughter before you whisk her back to the city?"

"We have three or four days, Mum. Thomas and John will be home this afternoon," I said, and she smiled, unshed tears filling her light-brown eyes.

Nothing that mattered existed outside of this family for my mother, and that was one of the reasons she and Elle got on so well. Mum had married my father quite young, and they had started their family immediately. She was now only fifty-four, and I sensed a growing restlessness about her.

When Lissie and Chelsea were in school, she passed time managing her flower shop, but she would give up the store in an instant if one of us needed more from her. She shared Elle's passion for art, and whenever we were home, Elle worked with Mother, teaching her to paint.

"Ben and Jessica finished up early with the US estate matters I sent them to handle, so they will be back today as well," I added. "You'll have your full house for the weekend."

She kissed my cheek before joining my wife, who stood gaping at the piece of furniture we had designed together when we were last home. It was a twenty-four-foot-long custom breakfast table made of Scottish oak that seated twenty people.

"It's here. . . . My God, look at this magnificent table, Will," Elle said. "Now we can all be together here in the kitchen." She wandered round the entire table, running her hands along the length of the polished wood. Her blissful smile damn near took my breath away.

And not a moment too soon did Lissie run into the kitchen and straight into Elle's arms.

"She isn't growing much," I muttered to my mother, watching the reunion ritual with Elle on her knees and Lissie clinging to her neck. "What did the physician say?"

"He says she's fine, that we should continue as we're doing and stop worrying over it. I've purchased the best organic supplements available, though he and I are likewise certain she has never suffered malnutrition. He believes it may have something to do with Isobel's pregnancy, but there's nothing to be done about that now, is there?" She added, "She will grow, William. She's thriving within our family and in school. Look at the happiness in her eyes."

I bent with my arms wide open to catch Lissie as she launched herself at me.

"Uncle Will, I missed you quite a lot," she exclaimed next to my ear, her words delivered with an ever-increasing English accent.

"I miss you always, princess," I said, squeezing her a bit too hard.

She grunted and pushed back to meet my eyes with her intense blue gaze. "You're getting superhero strong like you used to be. Does that mean your hurts are better?"

"Of course. Your auntie takes good care of me. How could I not feel better?" I winked at her, and she giggled while hooking her arms round my neck for another hug. "Shall we drive you to school this morning?"

"Of course," she repeated in the same pragmatic tone that I had used.

I grinned as she let go and slid to her feet. Lissie parroted Elle in most ways, mimicking her moves, the toss of her hair, a hand on the hip, the wrinkling of her nose. . . . So whenever she picked up something from me, however small, an overwhelming sense of pride hit me.

"We eat first, then to school," Elle said, taking us both by the hand and leading us to the new family breakfast table, where she had already settled Chelsea.

Members of the Six who were on-site began to drift in from

the basement training center. As far as we were concerned, those men were also part of our family, and they were welcomed at all meals in our homes. Christ, they were veteran soldiers and would always be treated with respect under my employ. They never complained about the back-and-forth between Eastridge and Kensington, nor about how much of their own lives had been consumed by the job.

My financial status allowed me to pay them well, and Joe Taylor was resourceful with scheduling personal time on a rotating basis. Ben Scott, who had served as head of my family's security operations for almost a decade, filled in for members of the Six whenever he was needed. But because he was my childhood best friend, it was rather difficult for him to shift his allegiance from me to my wife. And that was a condition required of everyone on my wife's safety team. I needed to know that each of Elle's personal protection officers would serve her, not me, and instinctively risk his life for hers.

Ben had a great head for property administration as well, so he also dabbled as my estate manager. It kept him close to home so he could be present for his three-year-old daughter. Ben's wife, Jane, lost her battle with cancer just after Chelsea was born.

Together we came to the conclusion that he should remain head of security ops but not serve on Elle's safety team on a daily basis, though he had come to love and respect my wife as the generous, loving woman who was helping to raise his daughter.

"It will be so nice to have Thomas and John here with us at the table tomorrow morning," Elle said, pulling me out of my head. "I can't wait to hear some of John's stories from Loughborough."

This young family, as unconventional as it might be, was my legacy. And at its core, sitting close on my left, at the center of our great breakfast table, was the woman who could make me a better man. She nurtured my soul, excised the demons that dwelled there, and guided me towards kindness and light and love.

We leaned in for each other's lips at the same time as if we'd been drawn there by some transcendent force, and after I placed a soft kiss on her mouth, she whispered close to my ear, "Our own children will sit at this table someday soon."

9

The next day came in a rush. I slipped out of bed without waking Elle and found my brothers waiting in the gym. Thomas was right. It was quite possible that I could no longer kick his arse. I had taken a blade to the shoulder and a bullet in the side several months back, and those injuries left me with not only scars but also permanent muscle damage. I had been at the top of my game, my strength incomparable.

John popped up from the thick mat covering a section of wood flooring in the gym, where I had put him on his back. "So you're a little leaner these days, but Christ, you're still a fucking beast, old man," he said.

I wiped the sweat from my neck and lifted my arm to stretch the weakened muscle tissue beneath it. "Careful, boy. Your tongue grows rather sharp."

His eyes dropped to the floor, and he mumbled an apology.

"Hit the shower, John. The three of us will talk about the ink this afternoon."

My youngest brother was turning eighteen soon, and he was anxious to get the same tattoo on his right shoulder that our father had inked onto mine. Thomas had the shield as well, as had Ethan. It was a Hastings rite of passage, but what was more, it committed the men who wore it to the pact made centuries ago between two families. Wearing the tattoo was a pledge to protect Elle's bloodline from reformations of the Order. In the present, the pact meant one thing—the protection of Elle and her children. Our children.

Thomas waited for John to head for the locker room before speaking up. "He's going to be a relentless shit about the ink. Have a think about creating something different—something symbolic but with new meaning that we can give to John and the next generation."

"It is a good idea, but do you believe John would accept something different than what you and I have? I don't want him to feel . . . well, less. Shit like that could affect his behavior for the rest of his life."

"We start with our sons, then," Thomas said. "I worry for John, is all. He's been shaped differently. He never endured our father the way we did. The way you did."

I gripped my brother's shoulder for a moment and shoved away the mental image of my father's fist connecting with my abdomen, one of the countless blows that had taken away my breath and had left me on my hands and knees, waiting for my eyesight to return.

Shame rushed through me. Because I never fought back. I had allowed my father to create another monster in his own image. Shame . . . because I had done the same to my brothers.

No fucking more. I won't punish them with my fists again.

"You and I will meet privately for about an hour this afternoon before the security team joins us in the war room. Let them know to be there, Thomas. And make sure no one misses Elle's brunch beforehand."

I walked away without hearing whatever it was he said.

I needed my wife.

Elle was in the shower facing the gray-and-white marble wall when I made it back to our bedroom suite. The length of her wet hair fell down her back and teased the sensual dimples where her backbone met her hips. Her curved arse widened perfectly from that point into the shape of a heart. I worked like hell to burn the image into my brain. It was another that I would use to block out the rest of the fucked-up world when the weight of it bore down on me.

"I know you're there . . . watching." She turned her head to meet my stare over her shoulder. "Are you going to stand there in your gym shorts, or are you planning to join me?"

"Witch," I said in response to the beautiful, mischievous smile on her lips.

My stiff cock and aching bollocks howled for a fast, hard fuck, but my heart needed more than that. I dropped my shorts and approached her slowly through the center opening of the glass barrier. My fingers burned with the need to feel her skin. I flexed them and waited for her to turn to me. I used my height to hover without touching, rounding my shoulders until she was confined within my space.

Our bodies were so close. I could feel the heat of hers reaching out to mine.

Warm water rained down over us from multiple showerheads and rinsed away the sweat from my body. We held each other's gaze, her soulful eyes diving into mine with an intensity that told me she could see into the depths of my ugly mood.

"Need you," I said hoarsely.

Elle nodded. "All of me is yours, and I love all of you much more than I can say. Touch me . . . please."

I skimmed my hands along her wet curves, and my eyes followed. "There are no fucking words good enough for you."

"No words," she repeated, lacing her fingers together behind my neck, pulling my eyes back to hers. "We don't need them. We'll never need them."

"Promise you won't ever leave me."

"How could I? We're bound in so many ways. I could never live without you, Will."

Soothed by her words, I let go of the past and the future. She was mine, and I was about to take everything from her to make myself whole again—to come out on the other side as the man she needed. The man who would crush the present to give her everything.

I moved in tighter and pressed her back against the smooth sheet of marble. I removed her hands from my neck and gently raised her arms above her head, locking both of her wrists in one of my hands as I pushed my hard cock into her stomach.

"Elle. I'm going to touch you . . . taste you . . . love you."

Her lips parted, and a soft moan slipped past them.

"Spread your legs."

She held my eyes while obeying my command, spreading those long legs to the extent that she could with the weight of my body confining hers, then circled her hips to create friction against my erection.

I used my free hand to force her hips still and growled a reprimand close to her mouth. My mouth watered from the thought of how sweet her tongue would taste when I kissed her.

"Do as I say, nothing more."

"Make me feel you," she whispered, her breath sweeping over my lips.

"Oh, but you will, my angel." My ego—the self-righteous bastard who had remained in hiding all morning—joined the party, and I smirked. "You'll feel all of me, and after you scream my name, you will beg me to stop touching you."

She knew there was utter truth in my words, so she tugged against my hold on her wrists. "Let me touch you first. Let me go down—"

I shook my head and cut off her words, the smug smile still plastered on my face. "You can do that later. Right now? You'll do as you're told."

Whenever she took me into her mouth it was mind-blowing, but right then, I wanted the first sensation that hit my cock and flowed through me to be the rapture that came with the initial thrust into her tight little cunt. Nothing would ever beat that.

Elle relaxed her arms and lifted her face to mine.

I claimed my wife's mouth, kissing her soft lips tenderly before leading us into a fiery, endless abyss. She broke the kiss. I lowered onto my knees and fucked her with my tongue and as promised, she cried out and pleaded with me to stop touching her there.

Allowing her to catch her breath would have been the right thing to do. But I didn't do that. Madness consumed me. I jerked her into my arms, seated her on my cock with a harsh thrust, and took all of her heaven.

10

I pounded my empty lowball tumbler on the wood conference table in the war room and jerked my chin towards the large, yellow envelope. Thomas had reviewed the contents a few days earlier at the office. He'd examined the photos and profiles of two men with potential to reform the Order, but he hadn't seen everything. I received another photo from an anonymous source by courier that morning, and my brother needed to see it.

Thomas dumped the contents and snatched up the new photo. "I recognize Isobel from Ellie's framed prints. . . . But who's the bloke next to Ethan?" he asked without diverting his eyes.

"Simon Parker."

He squinted at the photo. "You mean Parker as in—"

"That's right. The Simon Parker who was a member of the Order and the gunman who murdered Isobel and their grandmother."

"Shit. Where did this come from?"

"The courier had no idea, but he's been paid well," I said. "Flip it over." A handwritten message on the back of the photo was scribed in one of the old intelligence codes that our father had taught me. A phone number was revealed in the translation. "Let's ring that fucking number right now."

Thomas retrieved a burner phone from the storage locker. "Director Martin, you think?"

"Too careless for Martin. He would never courier something to Eastridge." I interpreted the digits from the code to Thomas. He tapped in the phone number, activated the speaker function, and set the device between us.

The male voice on the other end of the line asked for the raw code to be read back to him before he identified himself.

"Commissioner Brown here, Hastings. Is your line secure?"

"Yes, we're good. What is the meaning of this—where did you get this photo?"

"From your wife, sir."

"What?" I was stunned.

"My sister delivered it to me at the direction of the countess. Mine is a copy, as is the one you now have. The original remains in your wife's possession."

What the fuck? Elle had her hands on evidence so explosive it could implicate my brother as a potential traitor to my family, to me. And she had never shared it with me.

I had done well controlling my temper since returning from the States—to please Elle. But this time, she wasn't there to curb the anger that consumed my thoughts and laid waste to that control. Even worse, she was the trigger for it.

Betrayal hurt like hell, and in that moment, I couldn't reconcile the pain and the truth. My lungs accelerated, and I shot to my feet. Grabbing the chair I'd been sitting in, I launched it across the room.

Christ, I could hardly draw breath. I gripped the center of my chest as I fled the house.

I sped down the ridge in my car.

He betrayed me.

She lied to me.

Who was the true source of the pain coursing through me?

You, motherfucker. It's on you. You allowed her to lie. You created this situation.

Three hours and three-quarters of a bottle of whisky later, I watched Thomas pull into the otherwise-empty car park at the fishermen's beach beside me and step out of his vehicle. I was perched on the bonnet of my car, facing the turbulent English Channel.

It was her thing, looking out to the sea for answers. And that's where I found myself after driving round the countryside for a short time. I wanted to feel close to her as I sorted through my thoughts alone. The whisky warmed my blood and relaxed my impulsive judgment.

"You assured me that my wife's secrecy was harmless, brother. You might rethink your position before I ask again." I handed the bottle to Thomas but looked back out over the water.

"There was more to that phone call, you know," he said before taking a swig.

"Yeah, well, you handled it."

He leaned against his car, crossed his ankles, and took another drink. "Before we get to that, first thing's first. I know you're not going to blame this shit on Ellie. But if I'm wrong, and you tell me that is your plan, you should know that I'll break your fucking nose."

A fleeting smile crossed my lips. His instinct to protect her first in all circumstances was strong.

"I wish she had come to me with the photo, but I understand why she did not," I said. "Elle's just as fierce about guarding those she loves from pain as we are. She's protecting me."

"I'm glad we're on the same page then. Now we can relieve her of the burden."

"No, Thomas, we're not going to do that. She'll continue with her investigation, and we will clear the way. She needs this. Our family means the world to her, and if she's not permitted to contribute to its well-being, I'll lose her. We'll all lose her. Tell me about the call."

Thomas nodded and took another drink from the bottle.

"The commissioner is holding Simon Parker's younger brother on charges of international firearms trafficking. *Devon* is the name. Commissioner Brown spoke with Ellie this morning, and she asked to see Devon Parker. He said he told her no but promised he would interrogate Parker himself using her questions."

Fuck.

"You can't tell her no. She's willful. Saying no doesn't work. She'll find another way to get to him, goddammit," I said.

"The commissioner's not going to allow any harm to come to her, and nor will I. He'll continue to help her search for the answers behind the photo. He's already made her that promise. But I convinced him to report everything back to me. If she's in danger, you'll be the first to know, but I don't think you want to—"

"You're absolutely right. I can't be in a position where I'm trading lies with my wife on a daily basis. She'll come to me with all of this when she's ready. Let me be clear—it's you that I trust here, not Commissioner Brown. Is there anything else I should know?"

"Well, yes. Brown thinks Director Martin is the man to shed light on the Parker family. Martin may know the meaning of the photo. And it makes sense that he would, if you think about it. Most of his adult life was spent with our father—and since we know Simon Parker had joined the Order, you should look into it from that angle."

I nodded. Martin was already on his way to Eastridge at my insistence. I'd contacted him after leaving the house.

"I'll bring Taylor up to speed so he can keep an eye on it as well," Thomas added. "If he leaves her side for even a second, I'll kill him myself."

KISS FROM A ROSE

From: Ellie <ellie.hastings@hastingsgroup.co.uk>
To: Isobel <isobel.james@hastingsgroup.co.uk>

I learned something, and it may be the best shot I have to get answers to the questions overwhelming my mind. Your murderer, the vile man in the photo with you and Ethan, has a younger brother who still lives, and I'm going to see him. Commissioner Brown tells me that I may not see him myself. But I will. I need to look into his eyes and see his truth when he answers my questions.

You know me, Isobel. When I want something badly enough, I find a way to get it.

But there's something else. Jess retrieved copies of your medical records for me when she and Ben were in Connecticut last week, and the documents before me confirm everything I suspected. They also break my heart.

Your suffering was real, Isobel. I held you as you cried, kissed your salty tears, cared for you when you were broken. And that was genuine pain. I feel it again now.

The records reveal that you were pregnant, that the life I

believed was growing inside of you did exist for a while. But when Gran sent you away to have the baby after your husband left, you miscarried your own child.

I'm so sorry.

These are the only leads I have at this point, so I'll follow them as far as it will take me. I can think of nothing worse than what you've gone through, losing a baby you were already planning a life for. But it doesn't erase the certain betrayal that lies beneath the secret you buried, and I know that it must be uncovered, no matter the pain it causes. Your secret must be exposed. Because somehow, in the end—and I can't think how just yet—there will be something good that Will and I can salvage from the rubble.

Once upon a time, in a faraway land, I was the girl who cut and ran whenever she sensed something might break her heart. But that's no longer me. Not since Will came into my life. He is my salvation in a sea of devastation—the gain that God handed to me after I endured twenty-seven years of loss and pain.

That's how I know there's something worth fighting for at the bottom of this deep well of deception.

My family needs this one last truth set free. You know me, Isobel. . . . I'm going to set the damn thing free.

11

I lay in bed staring at the rings I'd put on Elle's finger. Her head was nestled in a cradle where my arm and shoulder met, and her hand rested on the center of my chest. Her long, soft tresses blanketed us.

The platinum wedding band was a delicate circle of diamonds, while the engagement ring was quite ostentatious. When I had designed it, I was determined to make it unique. Elle was in no way an ordinary woman, and a small, uninspired piece of jewelry on her finger every day would never do.

I lifted her hand and kissed the richly saturated red center stone, a rare Burmese ruby.

As often as possible, I watched her sleep. She would sometimes open her eyes and tell me it was creepy, but the tender smile on her face would assure me that it made her feel safe and loved. Goddammit, I loved her so much that I was allowing her to lie to me.

One of her soft, sleepy growls vibrated in her throat as she slipped a leg between mine.

"You're still here," she purred.

Most mornings I was either in the gym or heading for my

office before she roused. Elle was a restless sleeper, plagued by those fucking persistent nightmares. Her mind typically spun into the early morning hours before finding peace, so I could never bring myself to wake her too soon.

My brothers and I planned to skip the gym. We would get enough exercise outside in the copse when we took down trees and cut firewood for the house. Of course I could pay someone to provide the service, but it was a tradition of the Hastings men to do it together twice a year. We cut wood once before Christmas arrived and again before warmer weather returned. It was true that Elle and I were changing many of my family's traditions as we shaped a new legacy of our own, but this was one that we agreed would still serve the family well.

It was still quite early. I kissed her on the forehead. "You can sleep longer, baby. I'm not going anywhere."

My wife nodded, her warm cheek brushing against my chest.

These were the kind of moments she'd been showing me how to cherish. Each of her heartbeats, every single breath she inhaled and exhaled against my skin, was a gift to me.

Her lies meant nothing, and I would forgive them all. Christ, I'd already forgiven the ones she had yet to tell. Because the lies of an angel were never born of sin. Those false words—technically the omission of words—were meant to protect me from more pain.

I couldn't help but smile into the second kiss I placed on her forehead.

No one before Elle had ever protected me.

Her lies were quite lovely.

Two hours later, I kissed Elle's mouth one more time and climbed out of bed. She watched me get on towards the shower, her eyes drinking in the sight of my backside as I walked away from our bed. I grinned.

We had both gone back to sleep. I woke to her slight weight on top of mine and her soft, warm lips touching the scar just above my collarbone. I'd filled my hands with her arse and had forced her body tightly against mine. Our eyes had locked, and our souls had connected.

What are you doing, angel? I had asked.

You're mine, William Hastings, and today I'm going to have you however I want you, she'd said before licking the thrumming pulse in my neck and heading south with her lips and that wicked little tongue.

When I had been close to coming, I'd shot upright, pulling my wife to her knees on my lap. She'd wrapped her arms round my neck and crushed her lips against mine.

Elle had broken our deep kiss and worked to catch her breath. *Like this . . . you still have control. . . . But I want us to be just like this, Will.* Then she'd kissed me again before I could counter with a single word.

In that moment, there had been nothing within me strong enough to compete with the desire to give her what she wanted. I had lifted her above my cock and guided her down on me. I'd controlled every movement of her body, pumping myself into her, angling my thrusts in the way that would make her come. I had pulled her mouth hard against mine and captured my name as we'd reached our orgasms, mine following hers. We'd fallen down onto the mattress and then to sleep.

I turned back to her now, still grinning. She was slipping into her dressing gown. "Are you joining me, baby, or do you have other plans?"

"As a matter of fact, I do want the shower to myself this morning."

"Suit yourself. Can't say I didn't offer you another ride." I winked and she grinned.

"Go on, you naughty Englishman . . . leave me to my dressing room. Don't forget the photojournalist from *Vanity Fair* will be prowling around the estate today."

Elle would come into the bathroom to use the water closet and brush her teeth—and bend over once or twice to be a tease—before losing track of time in that massive dressing room amid the clothing and shoes her stylist had delivered the evening before.

When she passed through, she mumbled to herself, her mind already focused elsewhere. I swear she muttered something about what one might wear to visit a prisoner at Scotland Yard.

Fucking bloody hell.

I shoved my hand through my wet hair. Nothing could have prepared me for that.

12

Elle and Jessica walked through the center of the meadow towards the copse where, for so many generations, my family had cultivated different species of trees and harvested them for firewood. Elle waved to me. She hadn't noticed Lissie and Chelsea, who were on their hands and knees near the small shelter house at the far edge of the woodland.

I waved back and pointed to where the girls were playing before getting on with the task at hand. Thomas and Ben and the groundskeepers were helping me fell an enormous old beech who had done her time.

John, along with Joe Taylor, was hoisted up into one of the hornbeams, cutting back overgrowth that we would season for kindling.

A few minutes later, the beech was down, and I heard my wife's husky laugh resonate through the brisk air. It was the joyful one that burst from her gut when she was overwhelmed with bright emotion. I tossed my headgear and gloves to the ground and sprinted along the tree line to get to her. No way in hell anything could have stopped me.

When I reached her, she was tumbling through the foliage

with the girls and the four orphaned yellow lab puppies that John and I had picked up earlier that morning from the county shelter.

My brothers and I were given a similar litter of pups when we were young, and it was one of the fondest childhood memories I could recall. I wanted to give the same to Lissie.

Elle popped up into my arms and hooked her legs on my waist as I spun us round a few times. Sunlight broke through a split of trees and lightened her green eyes, turning them into a mesmerizing shade of aquamarine.

"God, what an incredibly sweet thing to do, Will," she said before smashing her lips against mine. "You rescued them?"

"I did. We have the space and means, so it's not a big deal. It'll be quite a lot of fun for the girls growing up with the dogs."

"You're wrong. It is a big deal," she said, then rewarded me with a more intimate kiss. The magazine photographer appeared from nowhere to capture our moment. Elle slid to her feet. Then, and as we watched the girls nurse the pups with bottled milk, she whispered in my direction, "I'm so in love with you."

My heart was struck with a calm that I had only ever experienced once before—the day she married me—and I didn't know what the fuck to do with it now any more than I did at that time, so I squeezed her hand and kissed the top of her head. "No words, Elle," I said against her hair.

Mrs. Bates called out from the shelter house, where she and my mother were organizing a late Continental breakfast for family and staff. "Come along, now! Hot coffee and pastries, everyone."

"But . . . I don't wanna leave the puppies alone," Lissie said.

"No?" I winked and picked up the basket that we'd brought them home in, holding it low so she could reach inside. "Round them up. We'll take them with us."

Lissie gently placed each pup into the basket, reciting the names of her pint-sized treasures. "This one is for Chelsea. He's small like me, but he'll be so strong like you when he grows up."

She smiled and wrapped him in one of the blankets. "We named him Wyatt. Aunt Jess says it means he's a little warrior."

"That's a great name, princess. And listen, I'm proud of you for sharing with Chelsea."

"Thanks," she said, beaming up at me. "She's like my little sister, really. Oh! Guess what? Grannie said I can have hot cocoa milk with marshmallows for breakfast today!"

Christ. She looked like Ethan had when he'd lit up with excitement over a lucrative contract. Her eyes. "Well then, we better get over there before John gets after it. I'll bet Grannie has your scrambled eggs and cheese put out as well."

I watched Lissie skip away to the shelter house and considered the consistent emotional growth she was showing. She had been through hell, but my mother was right, Lissie was healing. She headed straight for John and challenged him with a bump of her hip.

Definitely a Hastings.

Elle came from behind and hooked her arm in mine as we walked. "Ben just ran up to the house in the Rover. He said your visitor has arrived?"

I nodded. "Randall Martin, an old friend of the family. He and my father worked together for many years and were like brothers. He's the director general for the Security Service."

"Security Service . . . you mean MI5?"

"Yes, the homeland's Security Service."

"So this good friend of the family, who was not present for Ethan's funeral or our wedding, just shows up to say hello? Why is he here now, Will?"

"To recruit me."

She tugged on my arm for me to stop. "What? No. You can't."

I set the basket on the ground and took her cheeks between my hands. "I won't do it, Elle, I promise. But I can't burn this bridge either. He's an important resource that I need to retain."

"Is it the Order—is someone coming after us again?" She

clung to my wrists, anxiety passing through her hands onto my skin like a cluster of electrical pinpricks.

I kissed the tip of her cold nose. "No panicking, Elle. I'm not aware of any particular threats at this time. But I must spend some time alone with Martin this afternoon to feel it out, and after that, I'll share with you any relevant information he discloses. You and me . . . we've got this, remember?"

She met my eyes and measured my words.

I needed her to agree, needed her to continue trusting me. "All right?"

"All right," she repeated, the full force of her stare burning into me. "You know I trust you, Will."

She had an unshakable belief in me that defied explanation. Her commitment was genuine, but I'd be a fool to dismiss the sharp warning she layered within each syllable.

I needed to tell her soon about my suspicions or risk losing her confidence, and I would tell her after my meeting with Martin. My word was something she counted on to see her through the aftermath of the losses she had endured. And for fuck's sake, she was already heading for potential jeopardy with the Devon Parker situation.

"I want you to truly hear me when I say this. I learned a great lesson after you followed me to the States. It was irresponsible for me to keep you in the dark the way that I did, and what's more, it was dangerous. I made the wrong call, risked both of our lives, but I won't make that mistake again, Elle. We'll make those necessary decisions together. We're in this together."

My beautiful, strong-willed wife relaxed and smiled. "You're stuck with me."

"Nothing could ever make me happier."

13

Director Martin swallowed two fingers of whisky in one go and slid his glass across the table for a refill. "You're sure you won't join my team, son? You are a wealthy man. You can hire the best executives in the world to run your business while you work with me, for our nation."

"It would mean lying to my wife every night when I came home to her, and I won't do that. I swore to her that if she married me—"

"Goddammit, Will, it's time. We both know you were trained for this kind of work, and the Lord knows you have skills beyond measure. After all you've seen, all you've done, you mean to tell me you would leave an opportunity like this one behind to keep the peace in your bedroom? Think of the benefits, for Ellie's sake."

"That's exactly what I'm telling you. And as well as you know me, you should know that pushing that one fucking button will net you nothing more than my anger." I was doing well to maintain an undemonstrative disposition, but if he pushed. . . . "I will aid you whenever you need me—not only because you mean something to this family, but because at times, we'll each require the other's competence." Pouring myself a couple of fingers, I added, "But I will not work for the government."

Martin nodded and cleared his throat. "The determination that accompanies your commitment defines you. Your mind can't be broken, and your ability to compartmentalize is brilliant—the agency needs you. If I were your handler, we'd be bloody unstoppable. I wish your father were here to witness the man you've become. There was a time when he had questioned if you would ever harness your power and give it purpose."

"I doubt my father and I could have both survived this period of my life."

"You would have killed him," he said, his words having no cloaked meaning. "You're the better man, or you will be once you have children of your own."

In my youth, I loved my father something fierce, and I worked hard to make him love me as well. But Martin was right. If my father had lived, if he'd had the chance to force his cruel mental tactics and physical punishments onto my younger brothers as he had with me—his training to cultivate natural-born warriors—I would have killed him.

I shot my whisky in an attempt to dull the emotional sting and quickly poured another. "My father does quite well these days lying up on the hill with his father. Let's move on, shall we? Let's discuss the fate of my children, since you so kindly brought them up."

"Ellie's children, you mean."

"When have I ever spoken in a dodgy manner? Elle will never have children with anyone other than me. Therefore, we are discussing *my* children."

"All right." He filled our glasses again before meeting my eyes. "We'll avoid direct references to your wife during our professional conversations as best we can."

All I could manage was the slight drop of my chin. Christ, the idea that we even needed to have these exchanges was fucking me up quite good. I thought I had gone far enough to keep Elle safe and provide her with the peace she deserved. The goddamned Order had been eradicated and a mutually beneficial understanding reached with the Crown. Yet apprehension still gnawed at my gut.

With the personal matter settled, it was time to bring my brothers into the meeting. I grabbed my mobile and sent a quick text to Thomas: War room ten minutes with John.

"When my brothers arrive, we'll discuss our suspicions about a potential reformation of the Order and how that affects my children. But first, if you would, I need you to dive through your recollections to a time when Simon Parker's family might have been connected to mine." I tossed the copy of Elle's photo onto the table before him. "The commissioner believes you may know the meaning of this."

He eyed me warily. "The commissioner? You're working with the Met Police? That creates a considerable conflict for me. I can't—"

"Not me. Elle. She is friends with his sister. My wife is conducting a separate investigation in which I am not involved. She doesn't know that I'm aware."

"She's lying to you?"

"I'm allowing it." My tone was curt, and the price he or anyone else would pay for interfering in my wife's business was evident.

Back the fuck off or risk death.

Martin conceded with an indirect nod. He then reached for the photograph in front of him, but quickly drew back his hand. He studied the faces without touching it. "Oh, Christ." He swallowed hard and his face paled.

"What is it? Tell me what you see," I pressed.

"Your sister . . . I see your sister."

14

I shoved back from the conference room table and sprung to my feet. "What the fuck are you talking about, Martin? The woman in that photo was Elle's sister—Isobel James, the woman Simon Parker murdered."

Martin shook his head, the photo now held tightly in his hand as he continued to stare at it. "No, son. The young woman in this photo was Richard's daughter, your sister."

What the—my sister?

"You're mistaken. You know I've never had a sister." I went over to his side of the table, snatched the picture from his hand, and waved it in front of his face. "Look closer, goddammit. What is the connection here between Ethan and Simon Parker?"

"Calm yourself, William. It seems there are two separate matters to be worked out. Shall we wait for your brothers or get started?"

Martin was tall and lean. His quiet demeanor commanded respect, and he had a brilliant mind. And because he was a smart man, he knew that I could easily take his life. Nevertheless, my superior physical stature and aggressive behavior did not intimidate him as it would an ordinary man.

As luck would have it, Thomas entered the room with John close on his heels. Thomas gave a slight nod, his eyes revealing apprehension. He and I were rather perceptive with regard to each other's state of mind, and his visible concern indicated that he understood the type of situation he had walked in on.

"Brother," he said, reminding me to check myself.

I reciprocated with a nod, then pictured Elle's pretty smile. She was all that mattered. The muscles in my shoulders relaxed, and I gestured towards Martin's seat. "Yes, sir. We're ready to listen."

My brothers and I sat opposite of our longtime family friend.

"First, let me offer my apologies. This news should have been passed on to you from your father," Martin said, holding up the photo. "I can't speak to the notion that there was a direct link between Ethan and Simon Parker. But I will follow up on that potential business connection you mentioned a while back and let you know if that client was somehow linked to the same Parker family."

"Truth is," he added, "I'm quite certain this young woman in the photo was your sister."

"Our mother would never give up one of her children," I said.

"Of course not, but your father would," he countered. "The goddamned son-of-a-bitch promised me this would never come back to hurt Mary. I warned him that placing his illegitimate daughter with Edward James could become problematic given the connection between the two families. 'Two birds, one stone,' he'd told me."

Thomas reached for the photo and stared at it. "How can you be so sure? She doesn't look anything like our father. My brothers and I inherited his distinct features."

Martin shrugged. "You're men. She was a near perfect image of her mother. I knew her mother—she was an agency asset. We lost her to a mission six months after she delivered the baby . . . Isobel."

Panic beat through me, and I lost my breath for a minute. One word was trapped on my tongue. I would not say it out loud. I would not taint her name.

Lissie.

"Tell me Ethan didn't know . . . didn't know he was fucking his own sister," I said. "Tell me that my brother did not have a child with our half sister."

One could have heard a pin drop in the seconds that followed when Elle stepped into the conference room. She immediately stilled, her lips pressed in a tight line. I recognized the look on her face. It was a fusion of heartbreak, anxiety, and determination—one of the many expressions in which each of her emotions was a striking contrast of the other.

She heard me.

"He did not . . ." Elle finally said. She put out a hand to catch herself on the doorframe.

I was on my feet in an instant, gathering her into my arms before she collapsed. "Look at me, Elle. Breath in . . . let it out. That's good."

She followed my breathing pattern, willing her anxiety to ease.

"I'm fine now. I promise. You can let me down," she said after catching her breath.

"Are you sure? I can take you upstairs."

"I'm sure." She steadied on her feet and rested her palms against my chest. "She wasn't my sister, and I'm still hurt by the deception, because I did love her. But now, at least there is some comfort in knowing that she was yours. She wasn't just some random stranger our fathers plucked from the streets."

"But think what this means." I blundered through the words, doing my best to soften the blow for her. "Consider the implications . . . the future effect . . . for Lissie."

She shook her head. "We are her parents now. We'll protect her."

"She will hate us when she learns the truth."

"No, Will. I don't believe that. Lissie will never learn to hate. And the fact that Isobel is your sister will be of no consequence—not in the way you're assuming." Then she nailed me hard with those eyes.

My clever wife was holding one more card in her hand than I had.

"Explain," I ordered.

Her gaze burned into mine. "Isobel is not Lissie's mother."

15

Thomas slipped the photograph of Ethan, Isobel, and Simon Parker into his pocket before Elle noticed it on the table. "Let's leave them to sort this out privately," he said, directing John and Martin out of the war room. "We'll settle the remainder of our business after lunch."

My eyes were locked onto Elle's. She should have known better—no space existed between us. We were one, and we'd already learned the hard way that there was no room for secrets.

She allowed her hands to drop from my chest and stepped backwards until she was against the wall. I placed my palms on that same wall, one on each side of her head, and confined her to my space while taking away hers, making it ours.

Her eyes were filled with enough fire and strength to counter my challenging stare. My wife parted her lips, and small breaths escaped through her mouth.

"You had an anxiety attack, and you beat it," I said.

"I did. I can. Because I have you."

"Yes. That's right, baby." Christ, my cock was hard, and I had to force my brain to focus on the matter at hand. What had she done to get that piece of information about Isobel? I dropped my head close to hers. "Elle. What did you do?"

"Nothing," she whispered.

"You're lying to me." I brushed my lips along her cheek, stopping at the corner of her mouth, and pushed my erection into her stomach. That particular answer may not have been a lie, but I wanted to express what she already knew—that she would never get anything past me. Not for long, anyway.

She gasped, surprised that I was turned on rather than angry with her. Her face bloomed with the color of desire, and her breathing accelerated.

Fucking hell.

I wanted to thrust my tongue into her mouth and taste her. I inhaled through my nose and exhaled against her rosy skin. Her scent intoxicated me further.

"Tell me what you know."

She did not. Instead, my beautiful little drug lifted onto her toes and pulled me to her lips, demanding that I take from her what she knew my body and soul craved.

And so I did. I drew her bottom lip between both of mine and sucked, the sweet taste sending vibrations through my blood.

"There was a second DNA test," she said hoarsely.

I nodded and pulled her back to my mouth, pushing past her lips with my tongue this time, to take the bruising kind of kiss that I needed. I had to get it out of my system if we were to move on with the conversation.

Elle whimpered against my mouth. I lowered my hands to her waist, and we fell deeply into another kiss that was softer but equally impassioned. It was a plea on my part. I was begging her to keep us from losing our way.

She broke first, and we stared into each other. Then she touched my face in the way only she could. She'd heard me.

"You never opened the envelope with Lissie's paternity results. I read the reports and realized the maternal sample Ethan had submitted didn't match Isobel's blood type. There's nothing more to what I know than that." Elle dragged her nails through the scruff on my jaw. "I have no idea who the biological mother is, but I intend to find out. And Will? Please don't try to stop me," she added.

"If you need my help—"

"I'll let you know. You have enough on your plate. Leave this to me."

I would let her have it. She needed a complete win, and it had to be one she achieved on her own. Thomas and I would stick to our plan. He would monitor her activity and come to me if my wife were in any perceived danger.

"My resources are yours, baby. You know that. But promise me you'll be careful. Remember who we are. . . . We will always have enemies lying in wait."

My consent put a smile on her face.

"Elle, I mean it. You must understand that your security is no longer only about the bloodline. The money, our titles . . . these are things I'm forced to factor in now. You're a billionaire countess, and your capitalist husband is disliked quite a lot for his cutthroat tactics."

She kissed me. Her lips were warm and luscious, and my cock was well aware.

"*Billionaire countess* sounds rather obnoxious."

I grinned, shaking my head. "Of course you would take offense to the two least harmful words but to none of the rest. Knew that before it left my tongue."

"Will," she said close to my ear, her voice throaty. "There are so many ways to better use your tongue right now." Her hand slid down the front of my trousers. The little witch ignored my erection and went straight for the bollocks. "Or I could use mine."

"Now who's the naughty one? Just you wait until I get you in my bed tonight—"

The war room door slid open with its typical rush of air, and my mother walked in.

Elle ducked beneath my arm and stepped away, blushing. My erection swiftly deflated.

My mother smiled at my wife. "I remember how beguiling it was to be in the throes of a brand-new marriage, dear."

"It seems the Hastings men know how to captivate a girl," Elle said as she pulled my mother's hand into her own. "But right now, this one needs to spend time with you. We'll be leaving for London in the morning."

"But everyone is in the kitchen. I came to say we are waiting for the two of you to join us for lunch."

Elle was setting me up to tell my mother what my father had done—how he had betrayed her with another woman. It would break her heart. Mum lived in her own world. One where her husband was a hero, and in her eyes, he was a wonderful father as well. He never told her that he treated her children severely down in the training center. She never visited. He had made it clear she was not welcome in the basement when he spent time with his sons.

He had never shared with her the worst pieces of himself.

I would never do that to Elle, would never allow her to live inside a fantasy in which she believed I was something other than the bad guy. I wanted Elle to love me through every stage of my evolution, from who I was to the better man I wanted to become now that I had her. I needed her to see into every dark corner of my soul and still love me . . . to heal my damaged pieces with her light. And she did.

I need her to stay for this conversation. She's the strong one.

But she wasn't staying. She wanted me to give my undivided attention to my mother.

Elle transferred my mother's hand from hers to mine.

"Mum, we need to talk. Elle will send plates here for us."

My mother looked up at me. "No. We must eat with the

family. Shall we meet privately in the drawing room after the meal?" Her soft brown eyes held mine, and I could see denial and fear eclipsing the happiness they had portrayed over the past few days.

I shook my head. "I'd rather not wait. We'll sit here and do this now."

WICKED GAMES

From: Ellie <ellie.hastings@hastingsgroup.co.uk>
To: Isobel <isobel.james@hastingsgroup.co.uk>

We have more in common than you know, Isobel Hastings. That should have been your name all along, but because your father hid the truth, it was never who you were. He gave you to my father when you were six months old, and you became someone else. Like me.

Our fathers chose for us to live our lives not knowing who we are. But they are gone now, and we are free. If only you were still here with me. You would be my sister-in-law, not my sister, and that is okay with me.

Did you know, Isobel? You knew who I was, but did you know who you were?

The more I learn about your father—Will's father—the more I believe he had his own game. Richard Hastings was a chess player, and his children were his game pieces. His sons were the knights, and you were a pawn. He lost, though. The endgame is here, and he did not survive to see it.

I'm sure I'll dream of Richard tonight. It's inevitable. His motives weigh heavily on my mind today. I would much rather dream of my husband—the once knight who is now king.

You lied, and your lies will always hurt. You were lied to, and those lies are also a source of pain for me now. I don't understand how to sort through it all yet, but know that I'm strong enough to handle it.

Dr. Clarke believes my anger has cooled, that moving forward, anger will come from a place other than grief. As difficult as it was, I found a way to open my heart to the anger, to embrace it, and it became the bridge that is slowly reconnecting my pieces.

None of this means the anxiety will leave me. I may never be free of the panic that slinks around my neck and steals the breath from my body. So I will continue to thank God for Will every day, because he believes in me, and that's how I overcome the internal assaults.

I fear there is more to come from your photo, Isobel. I'm not convinced that learning who your parents were resolves the meaning behind it.

And you know I'll keep looking until I find the answer.

16

Director Martin took my mother's hands and kissed them after we entered the foyer to see him off. "It no longer matters, Mary. The girl and her mother are gone. He loved you, not her. That's all that matters."

She caught the single tear that escaped her. The fact that she hadn't cried or shown much emotion when I told her about Isobel was an eye-opener. Elle had warned me on more than one occasion that my mother was not the same naïve woman she had been when my father lived, and I could now see that she was right.

"There is a principle we live by in this family, something Richard taught us all, although quite clearly he abandoned his own declaration. 'Blood is blood, no matter the circumstances.' We could have raised her here and protected her. My sons would still have had their sister. That is what matters." She paused, then added, "I've never been a compassionless woman, Randall. I would have accepted his child into my home." My mother was grief-stricken over the stepdaughter she had never met.

Martin pulled her into his arms. "You are more than he ever deserved, Mary."

I lay my hand on Mum's shoulder and gave a gentle squeeze. I wouldn't allow Martin to take advantage of her vulnerable state. He'd always been attracted to her. "Elle asked me to send you upstairs to help her dress for the photos. She'll be waiting for you."

My mother then hugged me, but before heading up to my wife's dressing room, she said, "You gave me what your father did not. You gave me a daughter whom I love dearly. We can never lose her."

As if she'd willed it, a knot developed in my throat, and I swallowed to release it. I had come close more than once to losing Elle in Connecticut. I managed to spit out the one word that came to me. "Never."

Martin extended his hand to me. "Take good care of them both, William."

"Yes, sir. Stay in touch. You know how to reach me."

The director, my brothers, and I had agreed in the meeting resumed after lunch that there was no imminent danger with regard to reformation of the Order, although Elle's pregnancy would be the trigger if it were to come about. Martin and I would keep our eyes on the targets most likely to incite membership and recruit assassins. There were two men, unrelated by any obvious means. Come the next morning in London, I would employ a retired SIS intelligence officer to investigate further and surveil the suspected extremists.

After that final meeting with Martin had ended, Elle and I had walked through the gardens alone, hand in hand, and I had filled her in. I meant it when I'd told her that I had learned my lesson—concealing the status of our enemies from her in the past was a mistake that I wouldn't make again. Forcing my wife to walk blindly through this hell served no useful purpose. My woman was strong and tenacious, which meant keeping her in the dark only positioned her for greater risk.

During our walk, Elle had asked questions about my relationship with my father that I hadn't been prepared to answer. I could tell her only that his intense drive had led to proportionately intense physical punishments and that I wanted to be different than he was.

You're proving that with Lissie . . . and with John, she had said to convince me it was possible.

Martin placed his other hand on top of our clasped hands to pull me out of my head. "Since you won't join me at the agency, I'm quite glad to have our arrangement."

I gave a slight nod, and he walked out the door.

Thomas approached from behind, then, as I watched the director get into his car and drive away. "John and I are heading back to London. Jessica asked to ride along."

"What?"

"I think she wants to be close to Ellie for a while. Your wife told her everything, and she wants to help with Ellie's protection detail."

"She wasn't able to keep Elle out of trouble in Connecticut. Christ, Elle ended up saving her instead. No. My men do not need the distraction. Leave Jessica here."

"I'll make that call," Elle said as she descended the staircase in the white lace gown she had worn on our wedding day. "She's my best friend, and she can come to Kensington with me for a while. Let her ride to the city with your brothers." She stood on the last step and smiled sweetly.

The curve of her lips, the exquisite gown that reminded me how she had given me everything, and those beautiful eyes—she stole my breath and my heart all over again. My mouth went dry, and my heart missed a beat or two inside my chest.

Mine.

I had to track backwards through my head to revisit the words she had just spoken.

Goddammit.

"As your friend, she may visit Kensington whenever you wish.

But she may not get involved in security logistics. If she fucks with my team, I will send her back home."

"She will earn your trust and then your permission." Elle winked. "Can you go change so we can walk to the chapel? The photographer and her crew are waiting for us. I would really like to get them off the estate so we can spend our last evening at home with family."

I went to her, gripped her waist, and placed a tender kiss on her lips. "You are so beautiful, Elle."

She looked down, her long lashes touching the soft blush that spread over her cheeks.

I wished in that moment that I could read her mind. My ego sought assurance that her thoughts were of me and only me, while at the same time, I was filled with the warmth of satisfaction each time she blushed for me, each time she came for me.

This was the same flushed glow she wore on our wedding day after I kissed her long and hard in front of our guests. The bishop had declared her my wife.

"Thank you," she whispered.

Regret hit me. "You should have Jess with you if that's what you want, baby. Who will help with the girls while she's in London?"

The situation was similar to the one with my own best friend. We loved them both, and they were part of our extended family, though I'd been hard on Jessica. I was dissatisfied with the way she failed to protect Elle in Stonington. She was a good marksman, but that wasn't enough. She was unable to shield her asset. When she'd asked to become part of the security team, I had said no without hesitation.

Elle wanted me to open my heart in order to see her friend for the lovely and capable person Elle believed she was, and I would find a way to give that to my wife. I owed Jessica as much when it came down to it. She had medically saved my life.

What bothered me right then was the idea that she was

stringing Ben along. The day before, when I had mentioned it to Elle, she'd replied that it wasn't the case and asked me to let them see their way through it unless the situation blew up or Ben came to me for advice. He had not.

Elle's eyes hit mine. "Mary's shop will remain slow for another month until warmer weather arrives, so she can kick in more time with the girls. Jess can't be our nanny forever. It was meant to be a temporary solution. Your mother plans to start interviewing to fill Sue's position."

I nodded.

Thomas was standing there, still waiting for my answer. I watched him stare at my wife.

"Go on, then," I snapped. "Take Jessica with you."

"Fuck you," he grumbled under his breath and walked off.

"He's irritable more and more. What's going on, Will?"

"Nothing for you to worry over, Elle. He needs companionship."

"Companionship? Wait—do you mean sex?"

"I've warned him to use discretion." I kissed the tip of her nose, then headed up the staircase. "Wait in the drawing room for me. I won't be long."

Her stare burned into my back. "But . . . do you mean . . . with Jess? Is that why he said she could ride to London with him?"

"No. Your friend isn't quite his type."

"Well, what is his type?" she called after me.

You are.

17

As Jim Elliot exited my office with Thomas, I assured him of my brother's brilliance and wished him well. "We'll see you at the gala. My wife is eager to meet yours," he called back over his shoulder. It was a relief to see them go. I'd been spiraling into a black mood for hours.

Elle and I had been back in London for two weeks, and I couldn't say if her distance was because Jessica was there, if it had been caused by the nonstop rain, or if my wife was tiring of my bullshit, but I could feel her slipping away from me. As she grew distant, my command of her became more severe, and I tightened my grip on her independence. I began questioning her about where and how she was spending her time.

I need to clear the way to Paris.

I needed to regain our footing. We could reconnect in a new environment, in Paris, where we would be free of distractions, and she could trust me to be her truth again. The same way she had when we fell in love and when she married me. I'd loved her before that, but she insisted we not count the years I spent longing for her as the beginning of our story.

Our story began the morning of Stonington's blessing of the fleet.

That was the first time I connected with your soul, and you mine, so that has to be the beginning, she had once said.

Truth was, the years before that were like black marks permanently stamped onto my brain. The yearning, the emptiness, the fight to drive her from my mind—battle scars on my heart from the only war I would ever lose.

Now, living without all of her was not an option for me. The darkness of my mood intensified, and there was but a single means to stop it from becoming something brutal.

Spend time alone with Elle.

I grabbed my mobile and rang her as I walked out of my office, unconcerned about the remaining commitments on my calendar, leaving Sean to manage the resulting chaos. Thomas and James Jackson were there. It was their job to cover for me, and they were quite good at it.

She picked up on the fourth ring. "I missed you this morning. You left earlier than usual." Her voice was silky and filled with introspection, which meant she was painting.

"I know, baby. Board meeting. What are you working on?"

"I'm finishing Victoria and Albert. I really hope this modern interpretation goes over well at the auction. It's our first gala, and the foundation could use a boost."

Elle was captivated by Queen Victoria's love story. She often depicted historical leads as contemporary survivors in her art. It was no surprise to me. Representations of her own history were omnipresent in those same works, displayed for all the world to see, though people could only understand which of her stories she was telling if they were close enough to truly know her.

That excluded most people. Admirers appreciated her talent but sometimes interpreted the idea of her pieces with inaccuracy. She never corrected them. Instead, she would remind me of the bias that lives in all art forms. I understood that, but she was mine, and my irritation with the misinterpretations was driven by a desire for others to see my wife's beautiful mind as I did.

Elle was bold and reserved at the same time, and I imagined that was the reason she loved painting. It provided her with the opportunity to reveal her secret thoughts while her audience remained none the wiser about who she was.

She was the kind of woman who unwittingly tempted others with the promise of knowing her but left most with nothing more than an undefined craving.

The story she was telling now was ours—two people bound to one another by the circumstances of our births. We were, like Victoria and Albert, a woman and a man whose separate lives were thrust into one existence through the history of our connected families. . . . And like the Queen and Prince Albert, Elle and I had fallen madly in love despite the forced ties.

I stepped out of my car and stared at our London home. Large windows on the ground floor flanked the central entrance and created a warm invitation. The front-facing rooms on the first and second stories had exterior French glass doors and ornate stone balconies. Smart attic dormers ascended from a corniced parapet.

A delicate fragrance hit my senses as I entered the house. The fresh roses I had sent adorned every room. It was the first time I'd sent all red roses, a reflection of my anxious thoughts.

Taylor was standing in the foyer, his back to the wall beneath the staircase and a crime novel in his hand. He nodded once in greeting. "We weren't expecting you so soon. I'll head downstairs and give you some privacy." A slight smile marked his face as he angled his head towards the dining room. "We put Jessica on a train this morning."

"Good."

Elle sat on a swiveling stool in front of a canvas larger than she was, lost in the examination of her work. Taylor had relocated her easel and supplies from where I'd last seen them to the dining room at the back of the house. Elle drifted from room to room like a gypsy when she painted at Kensington, following the natural light as it moved through the day, continually adjusting the perspective of her composition.

A chestnut strand fell from her upswept hair and landed on her cheek as she angled her head. She pushed at it with the back of her hand and left a smudge of pale blue paint in its wake. The same color streaked along the hem of one my T-shirts that she wore knotted at her waist. The tune she hummed was lovely, but I couldn't place it.

I tossed my jacket and tie and watched without interrupting.

Christ, she was beautiful. I imagined her letting down her hair and how it would fall over her back. The blond tips would tease me, coming so close to her arse.

"'A love like ours can burn down a city,'" she said without moving her eyes from the canvas. "He wrote those beautiful words to her in a letter."

"'My desire for you will never fade,'" I added.

She smiled at our surrogates on the canvas. "You opened the book."

"I did. Found it in the kitchen. The original letters are preserved at Windsor. We'll take a look next time we go."

She set down her palette and rushed to meet me in the center of the room. "You came home early for me?"

Fuck yes, I came home early for you. As if she had to ask.

I cupped her face and kissed her lips, murmuring against her soft mouth about how I'd missed her and needed her. The desire to feel the instant when her soul mended mine consumed me and strengthened the intensity of my mood.

She locked onto my gaze and hooked her arms tightly round my neck, and I knew she recognized my desperation. "No words, Will," she whispered.

It had been several days since we'd made love, and I wanted everything from her, every fucking exquisite bit of her. Her love was the one thing I would get on my knees and beg for. The only thing to satisfy the hunger of my addiction.

I was certain that if she had rejected me when I went to the States for her, I would drink more. And I was equally certain that, had she rejected me, I would find myself once again ducking into the toilets to spike my vibrating blood with blow. Without her, it would have become an enslavement rather than something with which I had carefully walked the line.

I lifted her into my arms and kissed her again. She parted her lips to give me more, and all of my sick fucking thoughts left me. All of the madness slipped away when our mouths came together.

We made our way up the stairs to our room, stripping from our clothes along the way, and when our naked bodies hit the bed, I gave in to another kind of madness. I gave myself over to the power that possessed me to love her fiercely, to protect her, to absorb all of her into myself.

She moaned and writhed beneath my touch as I kissed my way back to her mouth from the feminine curve of her stomach. I couldn't help but smirk against her pouting lips as she pleaded with me for more. Nothing inflated my ego more than that, and it was the only thing that mattered. She wanted me as much as I wanted her.

"Turn over." I lifted myself so she could do as I'd ordered.

Elle stiffened for a moment, her eyes beating into mine, then obediently turned onto her stomach beneath me.

I smiled again, this time against the sweet spot where the little white birthmark on her neck called out to me. I pressed my lips onto her skin and held them there until her breath and her body relaxed. I slid an arm under her hips to lift them.

My erection jerked. I pushed it against her and filled the cleft between her arse cheeks. She arched and grinded against me, sending rumbling echoes of energy from my chest to the back of my throat.

Ah, Christ.

If she didn't stop that. . . . I needed to slow us down. Beneath her abdomen, I gathered her hands in one of mine and used the weight of my body over hers to command her submission.

"You are mine, Elle."

She stopped pushing me then, but not before slipping a hand free to pull my face round to her mouth—to remind me that she was as willing to give as I was to take.

"Please. I need you, Will."

I plunged my tongue into her mouth and tasted hers before dragging my kiss to her cheek, her neck, over her shoulder, and down the center of her back. There I kissed the pale blemishes that forever marked a dreadful period of time for us not so long ago.

Goose bumps bathed Elle's flesh, and her breath quickened as I trailed soft kisses along her spine in a slow, deliberate manner.

I worked my way down each side of her arse, making my way to her thighs, and in turn, she whimpered and writhed against my grip on her hips. Those mile-long legs quivered beneath my touch, and I ran my fingers and my tongue down them again. I closed my hand round her foot and pulled that leg up and over my head, flipping her onto her back.

I pushed my fingers inside of her to stretch the tight little cunt that was my home, dragging my mouth along her inner thigh, and she moaned the way I knew she would. Seeing her parted lips and hearing the hoarseness of her voice as my name left them damn near killed me.

I needed to be inside her, needed to be where she needed me.

And I needed to taste her. I withdrew my fingers and pulled her to my mouth.

"Oh, God, Will . . ." Her hands grasped at my hair, nails dug into my scalp. She came fast, breath bursting from her lungs, her pleasure making me smirk again. I shot up to her mouth with mine and shoved my cock inside her with a sharp thrust. Her throaty little scream filled me, and I swallowed it, the vibration reaching my soul, satisfying the emptiness—causing me to go still and search for control.

"I love you, Elle, with every breath until my last," I said into her hair where I'd buried my face. "Hold me this time, angel." She had already given herself over to me. Her hands gripped the pillow above her head.

I lifted my head to meet her stunning, tear-filled eyes. We maintained the connection while she wrapped her arms round my torso and her legs round mine. She traced a finger over the scar on my back created by the bullet's exit.

I kissed her neck where an assassin's hands had once severely bruised her throat. I had flown into a mad rage and killed that motherfucker with my bare hands.

"I get it now—I get why you pay attention to the physical wounds on my body, baby."

"It has never been about guilt."

I nodded, and her eyes cleared.

It was about time, not guilt. The scars on our bodies represented near losses of time.

She kissed the one on my shoulder, and my body trembled with the need to thrust into hers, to take everything from her—to hold her and never lose the time she was giving me.

"You scared me this week, Elle."

"I'm sorry. I didn't mean to be so withdrawn." Her lips curved into a playful smile. "Make love to me . . . and do it hard."

We grinned, and because I would deny my angel nothing, I drew my cock out and shoved back into her with another powerful thrust.

18

No one was there when I searched the rooms on the ground floor the next morning, so I hit the kitchen and rummaged through the drawers on my own. Elle and I had never left our bedroom again after going upstairs the day before. Mrs. Bates had brought up dinner, and we'd watched old movies until falling asleep.

"What are you looking for, dear?" Mrs. Bates was behind me.

"Another charger for my mobile. The one upstairs isn't working. Where is your staff?"

"I gave a few days gap. I can get on with things myself for a bit. The countess needs a break from the activity."

"You asked Jessica to go back to Eastridge." I should have realized. "Thank you."

"This is why I'm here, lad, no? To take care of the two of you." She opened the oven door and removed my breakfast plate. "Our lass has quite a lot of room back home to retreat to when she needs, but that's not so here at Kensington. It's up to us to send them away. Eat now and get on with it so you're not late this evening."

"Yes, ma'am," I teased, picking up a fork and a knife.

"That handsome smile . . . always been trouble . . ." she mumbled as she turned back to the range with her wooden spoon to stir the pot of sweet-smelling raspberry jam she was cooking.

Taylor came through the doorway and filled a mug with coffee. "Good morning, sir."

"You really need to stop that shit, Taylor. You don't owe me that."

"I'm a soldier. It's what I do. If you want me to stop, tell my commander." He winked and took a drink. "There was quite a queue for petrol at the filling station this morning." It was his way of telling me that his commander, my wife, was up to something without telling me she was up to something.

I gave him a slight nod. "Good to know."

"Keep a good eye on her—the both of you." Mrs. Bates removed the bubbling jam from the open flame and turned to eyeball me, as if to accuse me. "She hasn't been feeling well, you know."

She was right. Elle had experienced some headaches and bouts of nausea after we returned from Eastridge. I checked her birth control pills, and she'd been taking them as she should. Because of the type of pill she'd been prescribed to ease her cycles, it was common for her to go months at a time without a period. We knew enough to not assume the contraception was 100 percent effective against pregnancy, so she took a home test to confirm. The results were negative.

"Elle was doing quite well last night. She may have picked up a bug from Lissie or Chelsea. She tells me the girls often carry flu viruses home from their schools."

Later, after two meetings and a conference call with an investor in France, Thomas stepped into my office, headed straight for the bar, and poured himself a shot of whisky. "I'll be out for a few hours this afternoon. You need to stay in and focus on the contract you should have wrapped up yesterday."

He had shut the door when he came in.

"Stop with the nebulous bullshit and tell me what you're trying to say."

"Stay put," he repeated. "There's nothing vague about that. Keep your arse in the office, and close some business. My team in New York needs this win with the Elliot account."

I stood. My palms were itching. "Where is she going, Thomas? What is my wife doing today that has you on edge?"

"You've got it wrong. There is no edge. Things are rolling according to plan, and there is nothing you need to know today. Do you trust me, brother?"

No answer came to me. I trusted him, but I couldn't bring myself to reassure him of it. I turned towards the glass and raked a hand through my hair, staring out at the Thames. It was all I could do to keep myself from pacing.

Goddammit. I'd never had paranoia, but then again, I'd never had Elle.

"You need to say it, Will. I need to hear you say it."

I kept my back to him. "You know there is no one I trust more than you. But Elle is at the center of this, and I'm not sure I have the strength to hold back. I should call her out and put an end to it."

Selfish, weak prick.

"Think about what you just said. Has something changed?"

"What she needs has not changed."

I heard Thomas's glass hit the bar. "Well then. Wrap up the Elliot contract today."

"She won't stop," I said, watching Tower Bridge lift for a marine tug heading upriver.

"Ellie will find Lissie's mother, and she will stop."

"She wants her own children, which is why this matters to her."

"And you'll give her that . . . consequences be damned, as you say."

I spun to meet my brother's stare. "Would you?"

"Yes." His response held no hesitation. I noted the way he dropped his eyes to examine his watch.

"I'm no longer at the top of my game, Thomas. The injuries have—"

"You took a bullet for her. No amount of physical strength could be fiercer than that. And I assure you, I'm at the top of mine. No one will ever touch her."

We were discussing another war with the Order. The thought of a potential reformation fucked with my head, and I had to make it leave me for a time. Elle's investigation into Lissie's mother was more pressing in the short term, and something was going down later that afternoon that didn't feel right. It drove a sharp pain to the center of my chest.

"I'll sign your deal within the hour. Tell Sean to get me Jim Elliot on your way out."

19

I jumped into my car and followed Thomas's sleek Maserati through the city towards the Kensington house. My self-control was lost. My instinct to protect her always won, no matter what it cost me. No price was too high when it came to keeping my wife safe. Keeping her safe was in my blood. It had been beaten into me, and even so, I understood that my actions were now of my own choosing. My father could no longer force me to do what he had chosen for me, but this situation caused me to question the idea that I could change.

Elle was in my blood, and my brain was diseased from it.

Losing her was the only price that existed for me.

Thomas would realize I was following him soon enough. My brother had a brilliant mind, and unlike mine, his intellect and laser-sharp awareness had been freely developed, making him even more dangerous to his enemies. Innate instincts were unpredictable and consequently more perilous. Ethan and I made sure Thomas's skills were honed naturally. We'd covered for him, redirecting our father's attention onto ourselves. Thomas was quite cocky, and our father would have beaten the hell out him for it. All the same, cocky or not, my brother was the better man.

Thomas coasted through the security gate into the small car park beside the house, but he didn't leave his car. I watched from a distance as Andrew Evans, the second man on my security team who was also a Met Police authorized firearms officer, sprinted from the service entrance and got into the car with my brother.

I struck the side of my fist against the steering wheel. The plan was clear at that point. The commissioner had given in to Elle's demand to see Devon Parker, and Evans was Thomas's inside informant. Good—my brother left Joe Taylor out of his reconnaissance. That was good. He understood Taylor's allegiance had to remain with Elle.

But that wasn't enough to calm me.

Another Parker. Another threat. Instinct told me that since Simon had wanted my wife dead, Devon would want the same. My gut was certain about that.

Christ, I was allowing her to walk right into the ruse.

I accelerated and weaved between the lanes of traffic to catch up to Thomas's car. A horn blasted on my right as I cut back to the left. "Move, motherfuckers," I shouted. My brother's car moved swiftly through the traffic several car lengths ahead of me. He sped up.

My mobile rang.

"Go home, brother," Thomas shouted through the speaker. "Stop what you're doing before this becomes a bigger fucking mess for us all."

"He's a Parker, Thomas, and there's a history we haven't fully uncovered. Simon tried to kill her. Devon certainly wants her dead as well, goddammit!"

Another horn blasted on my right after a driver anticipated merging in front of me but was forced to hit his brakes as he realized I was moving too fast.

Ahead of me, Thomas zipped through traffic and headed for a side street close to Westminster Station. He made two left turns and stopped his car abruptly in an empty backstreet. He leaped out of his Maserati and ordered Evans to stay inside.

I sat in my car and gripped the wheel hard with both hands, my white knuckles aching from it. The pain in my chest intensified. Beads of sweat fell from my forehead onto my thighs. I pumped breath through my nose and stared straight ahead, refusing to make eye contact with my brother as he stalked towards my car.

"Get out, Will. Get the fuck out of the car now," he ordered, opening my door.

I shook my head and continued staring forward. "I can't do this. And I can't lose her. At every turn, regardless of the path I choose, that possibility stares me in the face."

That was the reality of the hell that I faced every minute of every day, and I deserved it. I had never deserved her. She was pure light, and I was nothing but darkness and ruin.

He softened his tone and extended his arm. "Christ. Come on, brother, step out for some air."

We clasped each other's forearms, and my brother pulled me to my feet.

I still couldn't look at him. I was . . . broken.

He placed a hand on my shoulder and squeezed. "You're right —we can't keep doing this. We're lying to her so that she can lie to us. That's fucked up. We've forgotten who she is."

I nodded. "She's tenacious when it comes to what's hers. She's protecting our family."

"Same as you and I would do. She's determined." Thomas put both hands against my shoulders and drew my eyes to his. I couldn't bear it for more than a few seconds. "Go home and wait for her. Tell her everything you just told me."

"I should, I know, but—"

"No, no more," he interrupted, shaking his head. "I've got this. No harm will come to your wife. You have my word. I'll text when she's on her way back to Kensington, and you will go there now. Be her partner, as you've said, not an enabler. That's the real win she needs, I think. Do you really believe she wants to be on her own with this shit?"

"You're right. Of course she doesn't want that." I gripped Thomas's shoulder, corrected my posture, and met his eyes. "She may even want me to blow it up and take the matter away from her. She'll be angry with me at first."

"Maybe. She does have quite a temper sometimes." He grinned and drew one from me.

"Go on, Thom," I said. "Be there with her. You make damned sure that she's not harmed in that room with Devon Parker."

A CRIMINAL MIND

From: Ellie <ellie.hastings@hastingsgroup.co.uk>
To: Isobel <isobel.james@hastingsgroup.co.uk>

He knows your secrets, Isobel. And now . . . so do I.

My heart banged around in my chest, sending a determined message to my screwed-up brain. There were no words at first because there was no question. Devon Parker was a few years younger, but he looked like his brother, Simon. His voice and his mannerisms were also quite similar.

I stared into his callous navy-blue eyes, and it was clear that he held the key to the locked box of truths that I was seeking.

Devon sneered. He was cryptic. He taunted and wished me dead, pulling viciously against the chain that linked the steel cuffs on his wrists and ran through the iron loop bolted to the center of the interrogation room table.

As sick as it was, I gathered the strength to confront Devon by visualizing Will's strong hands wrapped around his throat. Perhaps it was a foreshadowing of events to come, because I have no doubt that this man will someday meet my husband, and it will be the day that this last male Parker dies.

I grinned, and he tilted his head like a dog and called me a bizarre little bitch.

"Yes," I told him. "Because I know my life belongs to me. I will live much longer than you, and I believe you're sane enough to understand that. So, let's get on with this, shall we?"

Commissioner Brown pushed a small metal box across the table just short of Devon's shaking hands, and he said, "If you talk, it's yours. Refuse, and I'll give it to your cell mate."

I don't know what was inside, not precisely, and I didn't ask. I didn't care. I wanted information, and it did not matter to me how the commissioner extricated it on my behalf.

What mattered was that Devon Parker desperately wanted what was in that little pill tin, so he cooperated. His words were directed to the commissioner from that point. He looked at the photos I placed on the table and pointed at them to identify the people and recount what he knew about them.

"Are you certain . . . what you're saying is true?" I demanded more than once, but he would only respond to the commissioner.

He didn't meet my eyes again until the guards led him from the room, then he looked back over his shoulder to sneer one last time. "You've got quite some bollocks coming here, bitch."

I have more information about Lissie now, Isobel, though I'm not sure what to make of it. Knowing is one thing but understanding the motivation behind all the lies is another.

I know you, so I know that when you agreed to help Ethan hide your niece, your decision came from a strong sense of devotion.

But to whom were you devoted?

You were a liar, true, but a loyal person nonetheless.

20

I paced the length of the drawing room after sending away Mrs. Bates and shutting myself in, a lowball of Scotch in one hand and my mobile phone in the other. My nerves were raw. Turning my car and driving away from Scotland Yard, driving away from Elle while she was in the same room with a man who wanted her dead, was one of the hardest things I had ever done.

Never again. Not as long as I have breath in my body.

Words rolled through my head as I blundered through my thoughts to find the right argument that would make her forgive me once more, this time for taking back what I had given. It was a futile exercise, because in the end, words never worked for Elle and me. We communicated on some inexplicable plane of existence located in a deep level of understanding.

The nonverbal depth between us was something I could not describe. The obsession we mutually harbored was the reason we could leave out most of the common words and phrases couples often said to one another when conveying love or disagreeing, and that was the one thing I understood about us for certain. We were equally consumed.

Thomas's text message finally came. My wife was on her way back to me.

Another text buzzed my mobile, and I thanked Christ for it.

But there was no God and no son of God to thank. Not really. If God existed, He would not allow a woman so pure to endure the torment and loss Elle had suffered.

Reproach rumbled in my throat.

My wife would never agree with those thoughts. Elle's conceptually driven mind would instead work hard to show me the worth and magnificence in having a flawed God. She would do as she had done before our wedding. She would ask me to sit quietly with her in the private chapel at Eastridge. She would ask me again if I could feel it, feel God.

I would give her the same answer. I would say that I feel only her.

One day she might convince me, but that day would be when no threats against her remained—a day when she could fearlessly live every second of the beautiful life I'd promised her.

Elle: I miss you. Can you come home?

I replied: Already here. Need you.

After quite a long gap, she sent another message: Almost there.

The drawn-out pause told me she had guessed why I was home, and the two words she sent back revealed a combination of understanding and guilt. When Elle was angry, her emotions were bold and demonstrative. This was not that.

Fear took a back seat to the overwhelming relief that flooded my soul. I put my glass and phone on the table, sat on the edge of the sofa, and gave in to it, dropping my elbows to my thighs and my face into my hands. Unshed tears filled my eyes, and my throat burned as I swallowed them. Christ, I was a fucking wreck.

She has changed me.

"Will?"

By the time I wiped my watery eyes and lifted them to hers,

Elle was already on her knees, between my legs. She held my face in her hands and pulled me to her soft lips.

"Were you there, behind the glass?" she half-whispered.

I pushed my fingers through her hair and cradled the back of her head in my hands. She was unharmed. She was back with me. And she was still mine. "No, baby, I—"

"It was me. I was there, Ellie," Thomas said from the doorway. When we both turned to look at him, he backed into the foyer. "I'll be downstairs if you need me." My brother inspected our expressions for a moment and gave a slight nod. Then he walked away.

"I don't want to do this alone anymore, Will." She was shaking her head even as I still held it. Tears fell onto her cheeks, and I wiped them away with my thumbs. "I've hurt you. I wanted to lessen the pain, but I've caused you more."

Her breath quickened, keeping pace with the falling tears. As was always my first instinct, I gathered her tightly in my arms and pressed the side of her face to my chest. "Listen to my heart, baby. It's not broken. Not now, not like this."

"B-but . . . but . . . "

"Shhh, Elle. You have told me all that I need to know for now."

She nodded, and I could feel the warmth of her wet cheek through my shirt. "I'll t-tell you everything."

"I know. We'll talk when we're more settled." I stroked her hair and kissed the top of her head.

If she had learned in that interrogation room who Lissie's mother was, it could wait until we were whole again. Nothing would change over the next couple of hours. She was sheltered from the rest of the world inside my arms, and that was what we both needed right then. My angel had been trying to protect me, and I needed her to get that I understood. After all, I'd done the equivalent to her not so long ago. I had learned my lesson, and she was now doing the same.

Elle tightened her grip on my arm. "I feel his vile presence on my skin."

"Let's go up to the shower. I'll wash it away, and you'll never feel it again. I swear—never again, Elle."

And I meant it. I would never allow her to walk alone into a situation like that one with Devon Parker again. By any means necessary, I would make certain my wife never faced another man who wanted her dead.

She lifted her head and touched my cheek. "I'm so sorry, Will. I never want to be a source of pain for you."

I pulled her hand to my lips. "You could never be that. There is only one thing that can hurt me, Elle, and that's losing you. That fear is the reality I'm forced to live with every day. Maybe I hold on too tightly to you. Maybe I'm a sick fuck. But at every turn, the risk of losing you punches me in the face, reminding me of its power."

"You are stronger."

"*We* are stronger." I kissed her hand again.

She stood, leaving my lap empty and cold. The lost connection between our bodies was too much to bear. I got to my feet as well and led her upstairs to our bedroom, to the shower.

After turning on the tap, I unzipped the back of her dress, and she unbuttoned my shirt and trousers. The pieces of clothing dropped to the floor at our feet. Our eyes remained locked. I held her soul, and she cast her beautiful glow into mine, warming me, tempering me.

We stepped under the steaming water fall created by the showerheads, and I pulled her against my body, entwined my fingers in the long layers of her hair, and assaulted her sweet mouth with a ruthless, demanding kiss. My cock was hard and kicked out for her, but the moment we were in wasn't about taking her for my own pleasure.

Having an erection was a mindless symptom of being close to her physically and needing her emotionally, and I was working hard every day to rein in my instinctive desire to plunge into her body whenever we were alone just because I could.

"Turn round," I panted against her lips.

She turned to face the tile and tilted her head backwards, resting the top of it against my chest while she waited for me to fill my hands with shampoo and wash her hair. Elle gave all of herself to me as she always did. Every part of her body melted into my hands as I massaged soap onto her skin to cleanse away the obscure filth left behind by another man.

I held up my hands and stared at them. Devon Parker would be released from his incarceration sooner rather than later, and I would kill him. No other option existed in my mind. . . . And there was no question about how I would do it.

"Lift me so I can wash your hair now."

Her voice rescued me from the darkness.

Once she was in my arms and her legs were locked round my waist, Elle worked shampoo into my hair and massaged my scalp. My erection pulsed between us, and she used her hips to slide herself against it, creating an erogenous friction so perfect that my entire body shuddered with the need to come.

She used my shoulders for leverage to lift herself higher so that I could enter her.

I gripped the base of my erection, but instead of guiding it into her, I slid my hand up the shaft and squeezed near the head. A groan vibrated in my throat.

Pulling on my earlobe with her teeth, she said, "Take me."

"You were sore this morning, baby. I can wait." I squeezed harder.

"I'm fine now. We need this. Please, Will. You're close—come inside of me."

She crushed her mouth over mine, because that's what I would have done to hers to capture the cry she let out when I pulled her down onto my cock.

"Rather die than live without you," I tried to tell her as I pumped into her body.

I came fast and hard, too quickly for her to reach her own climax, so I dropped to my knees and drew it from her with my mouth. We collapsed together onto the shower floor. The cool tile soothed our overheated bodies while the warm water challenged the relief, raining more heat down over us.

Once Elle caught her breath, she got up on all fours and hovered over my sated body. Her eyes traced the large tattoo on my forearm that flaunted her name. Then, dragging her fingertips over it, she said with that beautiful fucking smile of hers, "Come on, savage. Get up. It's dinnertime—your wife is starving. And I suppose we have some matters to discuss."

21

She was dead. That's what Devon Parker had told my wife. Lissie's mother, his sister, had more than likely died somewhere on the streets from a drug overdose. He and his mother hadn't seen her in almost eight years, since she had given birth, and he claimed his sister was using both cocaine and opioids at that time.

Elle and I hadn't bothered to dress in anything other than pajamas after we left the shower, and we had asked Mrs. Bates to set our dinner in the drawing room, where we could talk privately away from the others in the house. Elle insisted we never spoil our bedroom by allowing in matters outside of our relationship. It was a general rule for her, and I was 100 percent on board with it. We needed our bedrooms to be private sanctuaries, an escape from the rest of the world, whether it be the grand apartment suite at Eastridge or the master bedroom suite at Kensington.

"Her name was Sarah Parker," Elle said as she pushed sticky toffee pudding round on her dessert plate. "Did you know her, Will?"

"I don't recall meeting any of the Parkers." I looked at the photo Elle placed on the table over my copy of the same. We had agreed to share everything—no more secrets or lies. "I wish I could say the same for Ethan, but clearly he did know Simon and Sarah. You said Devon identified him?"

"Yes. He named Ethan in the photo."

"We know what this photo means now, Elle. They were tying up Lissie's . . . adoption." I shook my head, and a pained feeling knifed at my gut. Ethan had done the same as our father had done with Isobel. "He could have raised her. Christ, I thought I knew my brother better than that. Why would he give her up?"

She put her hand on my thigh and rubbed there to soothe me. "Will, what if Sarah is alive?" Her tone shifted. "I will not lose our daughter to another woman. She belongs with us."

"I'll never let that happen. You've been the only constant in her life, and she belongs with you." I leaned in to kiss her lips, and at the same time, I was unable to hold back the smile pulling at mine. "Fierce mama."

The secret smile she shared only between the two of us lit up her face. "I have to be. Lissie is stubborn and energetic and brilliant, like you, and I'm sure our future children will be the same. Trouble will follow them simply because of who they are. And I must protect them."

For the third time that day, my wife healed another piece of me, eased yet another fear. She had no idea what those words meant to me. Our children would never live with the burden that I carried because Elle would shield them. She'd defend them, and she would save them from me should I become my father.

"Someday you'll tell me more about your childhood?"

Can't fool her. She damn near reads my mind.

I nodded. "You want to know more about my father, baby, I know. We have more pressing matters to manage right now, so let's shelve that tale for another time. All right?"

"All right. Another time, then."

"The investigator keeping an eye on the men Martin identified as potential subscribers to the Order can also locate Sarah Parker, dead or alive. I have no doubt about his skill. He'll dig this up, but you must promise to leave it to him, Elle. We made a deal. We work together."

"I won't break our deal. I promise. And thank you, Will, for putting the task into capable hands. I need to know Lissie is safe." She kissed my cheek.

"Me too. I'll get him on it first thing tomorrow morning. Let me ring Ben right away and get him up to speed, tell him to increase security measures at Eastridge and at the school." I stood and tapped Ben's name into my phone.

There was no way to be certain that Devon Parker did not have the means to communicate with others outside of his jail cell. We did not know if he had connections or if he was alone now that Simon was dead. And because Elle had ripped open old wounds, he would come for her, and I had to assume he would look for Lissie as well.

"I'll get Thomas," I added, heading for the kitchen, where he was having dinner with Mrs. Bates and the security team.

Elle was scrolling through her email when I returned to the drawing room just a few minutes later with Thomas and Joe Taylor. She pulled a throw over her bare legs and tossed her mobile phone onto the sofa. Her eyes were filled with concern when they met mine. Anxiety was pounding on her, and she was unaware that her breathing had become erratic.

I pulled in a heavy breath through my nose, making sure my chest visibly expanded with the effort, and she did the same. We exhaled together, and she nodded to let me know she understood.

Taylor and I remained near the doorway while Thomas went to her. My brother had asked for a minute to apologize before we got on with the discussion and planning. He moved a plush ottoman in front of Elle and sat on it facing her, his back to me.

"I'm sorry," I heard him say. His shoulders were slumped, his head held low. "I lied to you. I've been tailing you for weeks, hacking into your messages, invading your privacy. I regret not being upfront, and—"

"I forgive you, Thomas. You were protecting your brother, same as I was."

"No, Ellie. I was protecting you." He took my wife's hand. "I give you my word that I will not violate your privacy again."

Elle nodded and touched his arm with her other hand.

"You know, sometimes you forget that I'm your sworn defender as well. I yield to my brother because I respect him and for the sake of your attachment to him, but there will never be a time when I'm not actively shielding you. And your children."

"Same goes for me," John said from behind. I'd heard the front door and Mrs. Bates carrying on about something, but it hadn't occurred to me that John had already been looped in and would rush home.

"You received your birthday present," I said while keeping my eyes on the tense exchange between Thomas and Elle.

John cuffed me on the shoulder to grab my attention, paused for a moment, then hugged me with a wide grin on his face. "The car is great. Thanks, man. Is the art template here for the ink? I'm ready for it."

"Is that right?" I pulled his forehead to my mouth in a coarse action and kissed it before fully releasing him. "It's on the desk in the library."

John hurried over to Elle, then bumped Thomas from the ottoman as he embraced her and claimed the seat for himself. "Are you sick? You look quite pale."

Elle pulled her legs beneath her and smiled. "I'm sick of not seeing your handsome face around here more."

He grinned. "It takes about twenty-five minutes more to get here from Loughborough than from Hastings. It'll be easier now with the car. Thom says there could be more trouble. Do you remember our training?"

"I do, though I could use some practice while you're in town. And there will be no trouble as long as this family stays united."

"She's right. This family is strong, and it must stay that way." I sat next to Elle on the sofa, tucked her under my arm, and winked at John. "No more training unless it's with me, Elle."

She moved her gaze up to mine. "What? Will, but you—"

"I've changed my mind. I can teach you quite a lot more. You handled yourself well in Connecticut when you were in trouble, but it wasn't enough. You were too close. He would have killed you." I turned to John. "I want more time with you as well. Thomas and I have more to teach you before you'll be allowed to take your fight outside of the gym."

He had good technique, and he was fast, but he wasn't mentally prepared to fight with us when it came down to it. Emotional discipline was as important as physical expertise. What was more, he had to be prepared to end another man's life should he find himself in that particular situation.

Christ, I never wanted that for him. I'd given him a choice, and he had made the decision to be the last Hastings to fulfill the commitment of our family's rite. As much as I wanted to take that liberty away from him, I couldn't do it without breaking his spirit.

John squinted. "You don't have to feel guilty, brother. I chose the shield. And I swore to do as you say. I meant every word I said to you last week."

Elle jumped in. "Wait—you saw John last week?"

"Yeah. I took the helicopter up to the university for a visit. I didn't want to bother you with it, Elle. Jessica was here, and you weren't feeling well. With all the goings-on during our previous weekend at home, John and I never had the chance to talk privately about his path forward."

Her expression softened. "I love that you did."

The look on her face was one that I craved. Her eyes were shining with admiration and affection. In most instances, that look was the result of one of my selfish acts masked as a good deed. That wasn't to say my wife could be taken for an easy mark. Elle could see the wolf in sheep's clothing and understood my pretentious nature. She often called upon it to motivate me when there was something she wanted.

But in this instance, neither one of us got what we wanted. My trip to Loughborough pleased my younger brother but did nothing to change his mind.

John chose to become more like me.

In response to Elle's approval of my effort, and despite my own disappointment, the muscles in my face twitched until I allowed one corner of my mouth to lift.

"Let's get on with it," I said loudly after subduing the smirk. "I want to know that everyone in this room is on the same page before anyone leaves this house tonight."

22

Elle leaned over the iron and wood railing to soak in the view of the Royal Albert Hall from the gallery on the next evening. The London Philharmonic Orchestra's violin concerto floated through the air from the round. She had requested lavender lighting, and it created a breathtaking venue for our first charity gala, organized to raise funds for the Hastings Group Foundation Children's Trust.

She was breathtaking.

Her stunning floor-length gown was an exclusive, made for her by one of London's prominent designers, she'd said. It was light aqua—no doubt her stylist insisted on the color based on the venue lighting and Elle's eyes—and the neckline plunged deep between her breasts. My wife wore that cut well because she had a narrow chest with flawless, natural breasts. Her cleavage was slight yet sexy all the same. It was more than enough to make a man wonder what was beneath the dress while reminding him that the sophisticated woman he was eyeing was out of his league.

The lace on Elle's shoulders fluttered when air moved about her. I supposed the pieces of delicate fabric were sleeves, but there wasn't much to them. The crystal beading at her waist was finished in a similar shade as the fabric and was certainly meant to blend into the overall image, but for me, it was a beacon that led my gaze round her hips to the voluptuous arse that I loved to watch . . . touch . . . kiss.

Rather than restricting her long locks with an updo, she left her beach-scented hair flowing, the blond, curled tips dangling close to that fine backside.

"This is just fabulous." Elle turned from the balcony, and her bright eyes began to search along the curved wall to examine the works of art to be auctioned. "I can't believe the board members were able to get support from so many prolific and renowned artists. I'm not going to lie—I'm totally fangirling at the moment."

I pointed out her modern interpretation of Victoria and Albert. "Yours looks amazing. You know that, right?"

"I'm nervous about the exposure, but I'm confident in this piece. This is the first time I've had a problem parting with my own work. It makes me uneasy to think it may soon belong to someone who doesn't get them. That is, if anyone bids on mine."

"The auctioneer from Sotheby's—what's his name?—will receive many bids. I'm sure of it. Hell, I'd like to buy it myself, really, but at the same time I want to see it out in the world where others can appreciate the beautiful mind behind it."

"I need to let it go. That's what I want as well . . . to send them out into the world." She rested her hands on my jacket lapels and nailed me with her eyes. "One day, somewhere, someone will get it. So don't you dare buy it, William Hastings. Let it inspire another couple to love the way they did . . . like we do."

I had never been more desperate for anything than I was in that moment. Every part of me was on fire, burning for her, needing to crush my lips to hers at the very least. If I kissed her there and then in that way with the event staff fussing over us, she would blush, so I resisted for her sake. Instead, I brushed the back of my fingers along the length of her neck. Her pulse leaped against my knuckles.

I've gone fucking mad. This can't be my reality.

But it was.

"Say you'll never leave me, Elle."

"I—"

Before my wife could get the words I wanted to hear out of her pretty mouth, ushers abruptly opened the ticketed guest access doors, and VIP arrival announcements began. The event planner escorted Elle and me to a quiet room, insisting we shouldn't be present until guests had champagne in their hands and the master of ceremonies called out our introduction.

"Remember," the planner said, "this is the cocktail reception, and there are canapés stationed about for the duration of the auction. We're hosting the dinner for a more select group of guests afterwards in the private dining room downstairs. I will issue invitations to those who purchase a table during the reception. Please don't issue invitations of your own outside of the list you've given me. We want your guests to spend their money tonight." She winked.

"Thank you, Margaret," Elle said. "You've done a wonderful job with our event. Will and I are so pleased with the venue."

She touched Elle's hand for a moment. "It's been such a delight working with you, Ellie, though I do wish you'd allow me to address you properly. It's not often a countess with your lineage comes to call."

"It's quite all right. We have no desire to . . . well, endure more celebrity. We are grateful, of course, but Will's status in the financial community already casts a very large spotlight."

I took Elle's other hand but kept my mouth shut. I wanted her to take the lead with regard to our titles, and I was so fucking proud of the path she was choosing. I never cared about the earldom. It didn't mean much for me, but it elevated her in the eyes of the nation and served as a reminder of who she was, creating another layer of protection for her.

"I think you'll find there are many of us who appreciate that, Ellie. It's lovely to see Britain's young generation of nobility thriving independently while bringing the country into a contemporary era of peerage. That you and the youngest members of the royal family are so relatable is quite uplifting for us all. I'm not sure the monarchy would survive otherwise."

Elle smiled at Margaret and patted her arm, something she had picked up from my mother. Her smile was sincere and affectionate and demonstrated how she cared about the hopes and dreams of others.

Angel. Mine.

A knock at the door came then. Margaret rushed over and asked who it was.

"Hastings security, ma'am. I'm opening the door now." Taylor stepped across the threshold. "Please step out of the room, ma'am. I have urgent business for Mr. Hastings."

The event planner stepped out, and in came Director Martin. He had come dressed in black tie to blend in with the guests of the gala. Martin looked between Taylor and Elle and me.

"Go on with your sitrep. Taylor and my wife know what you and I know," I said.

Martin nodded. "I'm sorry to crash your gala."

"You are an invited guest," I countered.

"The Parker business connection you provided did not check out. It's not the same family. I have, however, discovered proof of what I believed all along—that Simon Parker's father was George Parker, and George was indeed a member of the Order. George made an attempt on Ellie's life nine years ago, a few months before your father's death, and your father took him out. I can't say whether or not Ethan knew about that."

Elle squeezed my hand. Her nails dug into my flesh. I pulled her close.

"My father killed George Parker. Christ, this changes things quite a lot."

"Does it? Remember, the Order was never a father-son tradition," Martin said.

I ignored his point. Because it meant there was something else.

"Will," Elle whispered. "Simon had said that he recently joined the Order. It didn't sound as if he had been raised believing it was his purpose."

"Did you get a direct indication or even a suggestion that Devon was involved with the Order when you spoke to him, Elle?" I kissed her hand.

Martin reprimanded me with narrowed eyes for allowing her to see Devon Parker.

"It won't happen again, Director," I said.

A combination of defiance and regret marked my wife's expression. "I recall nothing during my time with Devon that pointed to the Order. You may want to question Commissioner Brown. He has done other interviews with Devon. He knew exactly how to get him to talk."

"Could you identify Devon Parker in a photo should the need arise?" Martin asked her.

Protective instincts fired up, and I spoke on Elle's behalf. "Thomas was in the observation room to witness the interrogation. He can ID the man who threatened my wife."

Martin's attention stayed with Elle. "Did he threaten you in clear terms, Ellie?"

I waited for her to respond this time, because I needed to hear her say the words. I needed her to feel the weight of the words in my presence. She'd held back the exact language when telling me about the threat, "to spare me the image," is what she'd said. When Thomas and I spoke afterwards, he'd held back nothing.

"Devon believes I'm the reason for his brother's death." Elle swallowed hard, and I knew she was pushing back anxiety-induced nausea. "He said when he is released, he'll use his favorite hunting knife to slit me from . . . umm . . . cunt to throat and send me to hell with Simon." She dropped her eyes to the carpet. "I suppose that's pretty clear."

Rage thundered at the bottom of my soul.

23

Once we were announced and Margaret permitted us to circulate casually among the guests, the nervousness plaguing Elle subsided, and she was able to fully experience the gala. She was absolute perfection as she greeted our guests and networked with the other artists in attendance.

Our gala turned into something much larger than we'd expected after the first invitations were issued. Requests for invitations by community socialites and business owners then flooded Margaret's office. Because so many would be in attendance, Thomas had arranged for Ben and my entire security team, the Six, to supplant the event security staff for the evening. Taylor and Andrew Evans were armed with their Met Police–issued Glock pistols.

They're backup. No one will ever get past me.

"I need to freshen up in the ladies' room before we go down to our seats, Will. Margaret is calling for us. After you deliver your address, the auction will immediately begin."

"You sure you don't want to give the speech, baby?" I winked.

"No. Way." She kissed my cheek and dragged her fingers

down the front of my trousers as she dropped her arm. It was a discreet maneuver, a reflexive act to acknowledge the fire that always burned between us. "Besides, no one can command an audience better than my handsome, charismatic husband."

"Careful. Keep that up, and I'll take you into the back room first, lift that gown, and fuck the hell out of you."

I hadn't touched her since the quickie when we showered together the day before. She'd fallen asleep later that evening while I had handled a distressed client, and then she'd had another one of those fucking nightmares. There were more nights like that one than I cared to recall, and when they occurred, I would stay awake for hours, my wife held tightly in my arms while I watched her sleep and inhaled the breath she released. I had ached to be inside her then, and I burned for her now.

My blood constantly thrummed with the need to own her body.

Elle sucked in a sharp breath through her open mouth and held it, and I stared, waiting for her to exhale and say something.

"You've never said it that way before," she whispered. Desire filled her eyes.

"Are you offended?" She was not, and we both knew it. I smirked.

She had asked me to stop treating her as if she were fragile, and I wanted to give that to her but without going to the same places I had visited with other women. Everything was different with Elle.

It was difficult for me to inflict pain or oppression on this woman, even for her pleasure.

I hadn't hit her hard, but I was still unsettled about spanking her a few weeks back. With every recollection, my chest split. I had to show her that I neither wanted nor needed the rough foreplay. I suspected she was offering it for my sake.

"Offend me? Not at all." She flashed a smile. It was *the* smile. "And I love the idea about the back room, really. If all eyes weren't—"

There was no help for me, as hard as I sometimes tried. I gripped the back of her head and lowered my mouth onto hers, stealing the rest of her words. We needed the connection, however brief it had to be. Christ, I was dying to taste her. I slipped my tongue into her mouth and took from her the least of what I craved.

My wife didn't break the kiss as quickly as I thought she might, even when someone bumped into us, but when she did, she stayed close to my lips and said, "No words, Will."

"No words, my angel."

She slipped her hand into mine. "We should go. Walk me to the ladies' room."

We posed for the photographers in the round with the auctioneer and the buyer of Elle's piece. *Vanity Fair*'s photojournalist then followed us to the private dining room to shoot the final images for the magazine's forthcoming spread. The editor would contact my office to schedule our interview to complete the feature, she'd said.

Exhilaration continued to light Elle's face. There had been quite a lot of interest in her oil painting, and it had sold for more than double what I'd imagined it might go for. The buyer was a man not much older than me who purchased the art as a wedding gift for his fiancée, and that made Elle even happier.

My wife and I had squabbled in a lighthearted manner during the bidding war. She had challenged that it was her title and or my status drawing the interest, not her talent, and I'd argued the opposite.

Of course, I won.

The gentleman's fiancée had clearly related to my wife's perception, as was proven by her teary-eyed fawning over her new evocative treasure and by the pointed questions she had asked.

Taylor ushered the last photographer and others out of the dining room. Apart from him, Elle and I were alone, though it wouldn't be long before the highest bidders became our dinner guests and were shown to their tables.

"This is almost as majestic as the hall itself." Elle walked about the room, her fingertips gliding along purple orchid petals and fine linens and plush velvet chair backs. "That's Kensington Gardens," she said pointing to the view outside a large window. "So that must be the Prince Albert Memorial. God, it's so . . . ornate. It's odd that our house is so close to all of this. What is he holding?"

I leaned over her shoulder and wrapped my arms round her waist. "I believe he's holding the catalogue of the Great Exhibition. The history of the exhibition is in one of those books you have on the table in our library."

"Oh, yes. I did read about it. The lighting inside this room is perfect, right? It's the same lavender color scheme from the auditorium. I must tell Margaret how lovely it is."

"Yeah, it's quite nice. Kiss me, baby, before she gets here." I could hear the planner barking orders as she made her way through the kitchen.

Elle turned in my arms. I bent down and she leaned in. But the little witch didn't kiss me—she turned her head and whispered in my ear.

"Don't let me drink too much champagne. You know how it makes me sleepy."

And right then, before I could take my goddamned kiss, Margaret and her poor timing pushed through the set of steel doors. "Loves, let's have a walk through the kitchen. It's customary for elite patrons. You'll quite like Chavot. He's regarded as one of the finest French chefs of his generation. I do apologize in advance for his common swearing."

Elle grinned. "I'm certain we'll be fine with his use of language."

Margaret led us into Chavot's stainless steel domain. "When we exit, your dinner guests will be at their tables with champagne in hand. Thomas is receiving them at the door. Ellie, please take your husband's arm. The tile is slippery." She put out her thin arm in front of Taylor. "Please wait in the dining room."

"My wife's PPO goes with us," I said.

Taylor was the only personal protection officer from the team with a weapon on his person who maintained a close position to Elle at all times. Because shit would come to a head sooner rather than later with Devon Parker, and with Martin's findings on the history between our families, it was time to tighten security.

Truth be told, locking it all down round Elle was my thing, security emergency or not. A constant battle raged within me, and it grew uglier by the day, the mixed messages creating a state of mind that one may compare to madness.

Protect her . . . give her freedom . . . keep her close . . . respect her independence . . . imprison her.

I convinced myself over and over that what she needed was most important. But even when my hunger to own her was restrained, it remained close to the surface, unconquered, like a caged lion.

"Will?" Elle said. "Try this one." She held up a morsel of sea bass on a small tasting fork.

I closed my hand on her wrist—any excuse to touch her—and pulled the bite of fish into my mouth. "Ah, this is delicious, chef."

Chavot grinned and nodded. "*Un poisson pan-frit merveilleux qui est tres succulent.*"

I translated for Elle. "Yes, it is a wonderful pan-fried fish and it's quite juicy."

He turned to her. "You enjoy *le poisson,* Countess?"

"*Oui.* I like it very much."

I pulled him aside for a moment, and we conversed in French.

"No one other than you touches the food served to my wife. Understood?"

"C'est compris. Margaret m'informe de la situation de votre femme."

"Good. I'm glad Margaret informed you."

We tasted a few more of the evening's dishes at Chavot's insistence, thanked him for the cuisine he and the staff were plating for our dinner party, and returned to the dining room. The room now held a hundred preened guests in their black-tie best, all seated before extravagant place settings. Silver champagne chillers containing the finest vintages were arranged near the end of each table.

Another hundred and fifty or so people still moved about the building to take advantage of the gala's last call for cocktails and the orchestra's final performance of the evening. Some peered into the room as they passed to catch a glimpse of the private party their mediocre bids had cost them.

Thomas steered us to our table.

Elle grabbed my jacket sleeve and stopped cold. She was searching for strength. Her stare was locked on the massive wooden door that separated us from the rest of the hall.

Evans closed us in.

"No," she whispered with a slight shake of her head. "It's not him."

I secured her beneath my arm and pulled her against my side.

"Who, Elle?"

Small breaths rushed from her mouth, and goose bumps raised on her arm under my fingers. She wouldn't look at me.

"Tell me," I demanded, but she said nothing.

I gripped her elbows and pulled her to my chest. "You're shaking, Elle. You will tell me now."

When she lifted her eyes to mine, her pupils were blown.

The hairs on the back of my neck stood on end.

"I think I saw Devon Parker," she said.

MONSTER UNDER MY BED

From: Ellie <ellie.hastings@hastingsgroup.co.uk>
To: Isobel <isobel.james@hastingsgroup.co.uk>

As much as I hated the dreams where you were the villain, I now miss them. So many times I wished for them to end, for you to leave me alone. There were countless nights when I prayed for your lingering presence to be gone. But I miss the dreams. They were a connection to you, Isobel, and I'm mourning that loss.

And it is a loss. You know that I've forgiven you. Even with the lies between us, you were my sister, and you protected me, loved me. As I loved you. Why did we never say the words?

It's been more than three weeks since you've haunted my sleep, and I find the idea that you may never come to me that way again unnerving. A small voice inside me whispers that I'm losing you, this time for good.

I tell myself you're already gone, because you've been gone from the moment you died holding my hand. It's silly how I try to convince myself of things that I know my brain won't accept. I understand that you're not gone from my heart, but I do feel your spirit slipping away from me. Are you visiting someone else's dreams?

Someone else has come to mine.

For months, I dreamed of Simon Parker. The nightmares were all the same, with his sickening face in focus and everything else relegated to a dark abyss. Everything except for the silhouette of my body and my eyes. How strange that I could see the fear in my own eyes. I was tied to the posts of a metal bed that I did not recognize. He would touch me, cut the clothes from my body, push his fingers between my legs, and eventually drag them up to my throat, where he would wrap his calloused hands around my neck. He would choke me until I was close to death, but in the end, he took my life with a large knife.

That same dream has come back to me.

I do not share the contents of the nightmare with Will. You are the first to whom I've said these words. Will knows there are nightmares and who stars in them. He knows each one is horrifying, and he is the only person who can help me through the aftermath of these night terrors.

But there is no way that I will paint this picture for him. It would crush him, send him deeper into his own darkness.

He understands my suffering, my needs, my desires. He gets that I push him even when I know better because I need for us to feel more. Will knows that we need to go to the place where our souls are free to feel pain and love and fire and acceptance. He knows it's how we survive.

But if he were to imagine the gruesome visions driven into my head during the nightmares, the beast dwelling within his depths would command him to protect me from these terrors, and in turn, he would unintentionally take away the soulful connection that makes us one, through which we are free.

I tell you all of this, Isobel, because I find myself considering whether the nightmares are conjured images that are not real—

or if they are a warning of something to come. Now that I've met Devon Parker and he has described his death wish for me, I wonder if it's actually his face that I see in those cruel dreams.

24

The whimper that came from the back of Elle's throat was imperceptible to most, but not to me. She squeezed my hand. We stood in the middle of a private dinner party among event staff and the highest bidders from the foundation's charitable art auction, powerless to react without drawing unwanted attention.

"I'm not crazy, Will. I did see something," she whispered.

"I believe you, baby. I will always believe you." Of course she'd seen something. Elle had an extraordinary sense about this type of thing. Maybe it was the result of my own questionable behavior from a time not so long ago when I watched her from the shadows and followed her about town like some fucking stalker.

Perhaps that's what I had been. Her stalker.

"We need to be discreet in the way we address this here and now, but I promise you, Elle, we will address it."

Thomas was watching. He knew something was wrong with my wife. I met his gaze and angled my head in a slight gesture to bring him over to me.

"Contact the commissioner, and make certain Devon Parker is still behind bars. Now."

"Christ. Yes, right away." Thomas touched his earpiece and told Andrew Evans to make the call and then meet him in the alcove that housed the steel doors to the kitchen and a service exit from the dining room to the auditorium. He looked at Elle. "What happened?"

She stumbled through her words. "His face . . . I don't know. I thought . . . I swear it was his face. Before Andrew closed the door."

My brother redirected his attention to me. "Evans and I are able to identify Parker. We'll search the property, and I'll run by the security office to push the video feed out to my own server. We can meet later at Kensington to review the footage. You keep Taylor close, and do not leave this room without me."

I nodded. "Go."

Taylor stood with his back to a wall that divided the dining room from the alcove, no more than thirty-five feet from our table. He was instinctively in tune with Elle's distress. His posture signaled he was on high-alert status without a word from anyone.

Thomas moved across the room and waved Taylor into the alcove with Evans to provide both men with direction, then he and Evans disappeared into the building.

It pained me to stand down while my brother handled the situation, and it had nothing to do with trust, because I'd come to trust him like no other. Suppressing the impulse to pursue once you've been a hunter was challenging. And not being the one to physically clear the field for Elle's protection was even more difficult. It had always been my purpose, the reason for my existence.

Memories of my father flooded through me, the goddamned things stinging my heart like salt rubbed into an open wound. I blinked to get rid of them, but one remained.

I had been seventeen at the time.

Get up, soldier, my father had said, getting to his feet and watching me get to mine. He had been hovering over me on his knees, his large hands pinning my shoulders to the mat on the training-room floor. The force of his kick to the center of my chest had put me on my back.

Tell me again who you are, he had ordered, pointing to his eye.

I had pulled myself up to stand before him with my back straight and had locked my eyes into his. *I am a Hastings warrior, sir, and I'm the best there's ever been.* I had infused my voice with more power that time to please him. By then, my ego had begun taking on a life of its own. The inclusion of my sanctimonious declaration about being the best had been a risk but one that had paid in the end.

I will wear the shield and keep the girl safe from her enemies, I had added.

You will keep the girl safe from our *enemies when I tell you the time has arrived.*

Our enemies . . . when the time comes, sir.

My father's stern expression had become an unexpected grin, and he had winked at me. *Quite right. In the years to come, no one will beat you. But always remember, son, being the best fighter isn't enough. Your skill must come from here*—he had pounded on his chest, then pointed to his head—*and here as well.*

I had loved my father on that day.

Now that Elle and I were married, and now that I loved her the way that I did, my place was at her side. Leaving her to pursue and fight only created more vulnerabilities. I was no longer my family's field soldier. At some point after we returned from Connecticut, my brother had taken the position from me, and I had let him.

"Will, should we go home?"

Anger stirred inside of me. I had no idea what the fuck was

happening or who she had seen, but one thing was clear. No one was going to take this night away from her.

I pulled out her chair. "We'll stay. This will not ruin our evening."

She released her breath and summoned a cordial smile. "Of course, you're right. These people donated huge amounts of money to be here. They deserve a wonderful dinner party."

"It's you who deserves this dinner party."

As Elle took her seat, she looked up at me from beneath her long, dark lashes and nodded. The smile on her face changed then, transforming into one that was warmer, more genuine. She released another weighted exhale. Self-assured green eyes beat into mine.

I dragged my chair closer to hers and sat. She leaned into me and said, "Take what's ours, Will."

Christ.

Her determination was merciless when it surfaced. It devastated everything in its path.

The first time she'd told me to take what was ours had astonished me, and this was no different. The narcissism in me was rather complacent again, and she was manipulating it to get me back on track. It was the worst piece of me, but we both understood it was something we needed in order to survive the hateful shit that pursued us. The good news was, she was as talented at taming that part of me as she was at manipulating it.

She's a beautiful little force of nature.

I kissed her lips. "There are no words."

"I know," she said.

Margaret crouched behind our chairs and tapped my shoulder. "Mr. Hastings, now you'll thank your supporters one more time. Plates will be served, and the evening will finish with casual conversation. You should leave before the guests."

"Gladly. I think we've had quite enough. Do you need me to say something in particular?"

"You're an authoritative speaker, and you would do well to not listen to me this once." Margaret winked at me, then drew Elle's hand into hers. "It's been a pleasure, Ellie. You are a dear. I will contact you in the coming week to tie up loose ends. The account manager at Sotheby's will also reach out with confirmed numbers."

While we watched our event planner vanish beyond the alcove to take her leave, my mobile buzzed with Thomas's text message:

Private exit path secured. Ben inspecting car. Wait for me.

Elle and I made our way through the narrow corridors of the nonpublic access areas that Thomas had cleared. I was at her right side, and she held my left hand. Thomas was positioned on her left, Taylor was in front, and Evans walked close behind us.

The other four men from my security team were positioned strategically along the secure passageway created for our private exit to the car. Elle said good night to each man as we passed, using their first names, and I nodded and thanked them.

"The commissioner confirmed that Devon Parker is still locked up at Scotland Yard," my brother said.

"Do you trust that he put his own eyes on Parker?"

Thomas handed me his mobile. It displayed a photo of Parker in his jail cell, sent from the commissioner's personal phone number.

Elle abruptly turned her head away. Her nails pushed into the flesh of my palm.

I focused on Parker's face, learning every feature, every contour, every line. It was the face of a dead man, the face of my last hunt. My brother would argue for the kill, but this one was mine. One final ghost to join the others who haunted me.

Christ, he looked quite like his brother, Simon.

Simon Parker had killed what was left of Elle's family. He had killed . . . my sister. The vile motherfucker put a bullet through her heart. And he would have done the same to Elle if we hadn't found her that night when we did, before he could make his final move. Josh Mendes took that execution from me.

No one will take this one.

I handed the phone back to Thomas. "We need an update on his imprisonment status and the weapons trafficking charges. We don't even know if he's going to be convicted. I will hear it from Commissioner Brown myself." I pulled out my own mobile from my jacket pocket and sent a quick text message to my assistant. "Sean will get him to my office first thing. Be there, Thomas."

I lowered my chin and caught the question in my wife's eyes. She wanted to be there. I nodded to let her know that I was giving that to her. There was no reason for me to force her back into the dark. We had no more secrets. We were telling no more lies.

Elle rested the side of her face against my shoulder when we stopped at the end of the corridor, where the steel exit door before us announced our impending freedom. It seemed as if we'd been inside the hall for weeks rather than hours. I kissed the top of her head.

"Wait here for a minute, sir. I realize the car has been cleared, but still—my cargo, my inspection." Taylor maintained an assertive position when it came to Elle's safety.

Who could argue with that?

"Take care of it. We'll wait." I pulled his cargo into my arms and buried my nose in her hair. I drew in the familiar scent, but this time an additional floral note hit back. "New shampoo, Elle?"

"Sea salt and orchid oil," she mumbled into my jacket.

I strengthened my embrace and inhaled the scent again. My cock came to attention straightaway. "It's lovely . . . and my new favorite."

She nodded. "My feet are tired of these gorgeous Louboutins. I can't wait to get out of this gown."

"Come on now, baby . . . no teasing."

I pressed my erection into her stomach. Her head popped up from my chest. I winked.

"Remember what I said earlier?"

A little gasp rushed out of her mouth. She remembered.

In a flash, my lips were on hers, and my tongue was fucking her mouth. It was one of those transient moments within a captive span of time that she'd taught me to seize.

We were newlyweds for Christ's sake, yet so much of our time was spent either surrounded by other people or apart from each other. I was sick to fucking death of it, and right then, I didn't care who was standing there to see me kiss my wife. I needed to kiss her.

We needed Paris.

Taylor returned a few minutes later. "Change of plans," he said.

25

Thomas shook his head, not in disagreement, but in anger and disbelief. Several staff members from the on-site security department for the Royal Albert Hall had nosed round our car. The three men claimed that management directed them to assist with securing our safe departure.

"I told you arseholes to stay away from this area," Thomas shouted. "I don't give a goddamned fuck what your boss said at your meeting. . . . We made it clear that you were to defer 100 percent to this team tonight. None of you is qualified to participate in this protection detail." He grabbed one outspoken man by the collar. "Take your mates and get the fuck away from here while you can still walk away."

The security staffers recoiled from my brother's severe reprimand and hurried to leave us.

"Ben was confronting the loud one when I stepped out," Joe Taylor said to Elle and me. "But the other two . . . who the hell knows what they were doing. One was on his mobile. It's possible he dispatched information to paparazzi or someone else, and the city is humming with activity tonight. I prefer the countess not ride home in the Bentley, sir. One of the other cars has passed inspection, and we're ready when you are."

He made a sharp whistling sound, and the rest of the Six fell into position, harboring us within the refuge of their small paramilitary brigade.

I nodded. "That's good work, Taylor. My wife's tired. . . . Let's get her home."

Elle was resting her face against my chest again. She straightened, dropped her arms from my waist, and slipped her hand into mine. "Any delays, Joe?"

"There's quite a lot of traffic this evening, ma'am, but we'll have you home in fifteen minutes."

Beautiful green eyes narrowed on the word *ma'am,* and he smiled warmly. Taylor generally called her Ellie as she preferred, but never in public settings.

When we stepped outside into the night, brisk air hit our faces, relief surged through my lungs, and the tautness afflicting the muscles in my shoulders diminished.

"Look at the stars, Will. Can you feel their light touching your skin?" Elle shivered from the cold, closed her eyes, and lifted her chin higher towards the clear evening sky. Her breath decelerated, and little clouds of condensation escaped from between her parted lips.

Embracing the way she regarded all the temporal joys in life was easy because it was a beautiful thing to see. She openly celebrated the little things that most people took for granted, like warm rays of sunlight, whispered messages from the sea, the moodiness of the moon, and the stars. But her bright spirit was the only light that mattered to me, and nothing otherwise in the universe could affect my desire to live or to feel—not in the way that she did.

I smiled and watched her, choosing not to answer her question. I didn't want to tell her that I couldn't feel the stars, that her own brilliance hid their light from me. She would frown.

"You're changing," Ben said after Elle was inside the car.

I shrugged. "I don't want to be like him anymore."

"You've never been like your father. It's time you understood that, my brother."

Ease that hadn't existed between us for a couple of months settled in the air. Ben was my closest friend, and he had been since we were twelve-year-olds brought together by our fathers' shared ambition to train their sons. He was like a brother, really. Even so, we'd drifted apart.

A few days after the wedding, Ben and I argued about him leaving the estate. Elle stepped in and convinced him to reconsider his position. He swore to her his thoughts of moving out had nothing to do with his uncertain relationship with Jess, and he vowed to stay as long as he was a single father.

Elle was, after all, one of the women helping to raise his daughter. Whenever we were home, it was quite easy to see how Chelsea loved Elle and competed for her attention.

Eastridge was Ben's home and had been for many years, but in the end, if it was what he wanted, I would let him move on with his life.

"Time will tell." I clutched his shoulder for a second before ducking into the back of the car. "Glad you're here, my brother."

"Where else would I be," he said with a sly grin.

As we drove away from the event hall, I pulled my wife's long legs over my lap and wrapped her in my jacket and my arms. Elle made quick work of sliding out of her stiletto heels before I could get to her feet. She released my bow tie and lay her head on my shoulder.

I dropped my head backwards against the seat of the Range Rover and closed my eyes. "I'm going to run through the video footage tonight, but you should go to bed, baby."

I had to see. I couldn't go to bed without knowing what she saw.

"I can do it with you."

"Yeah, of course, I know. Thomas and I need to go through and tag the appropriate time frame, but that may take a while to sort out. You and I will review it together in the morning before we meet the commissioner."

"I don't want to sleep without you." Her whispered tone triggered the protective impulse waiting at the bottom of my gut. She was scared.

"You're having nightmares that you haven't told me about."

"I've not been lying," she snapped. "It's just that I don't want to worry you . . . because there's nothing to be done about it. My head is my head, and even you can't make that better."

I jerked upright and caught her chin with my forefinger so I could see her eyes. Christ, she'd never snapped at me like that. "What is it I'm missing here? And since when do we not soothe each other's mind?"

Tears and regret flooded her eyes.

"Talk to me, Elle."

"I'm sorry. I don't know why I said that. You don't deserve to be spoken to that way." She pushed her gaze higher into mine. "The dreams are the same, Will. Always the same. But, God, what if it's not Simon Parker's face that I see—what if it's Devon's face?"

"Devon Parker will never touch you."

The tears spilled down her cheeks. "You're planning to kill him."

"Yes."

"When did you know?"

"The day you went to see him in jail, he became a dead man walking. There's no way I can let him live. You know who I am, Elle, and you know there is no other way round this for me."

Her head moved up and down in a slight, corroborating gesture. "I really thought the worst was over for us, that we could be happy and normal and have a family." She sniffed and wiped at the watery fear rolling down her face. I caught as many tears with my thumbs as she allowed. "I mean, I know we have a family now, but we deserve to add to it. We deserve to have our own children."

"We will have that—I promise you we'll have it. There is time, Elle." A charged wave of angst ripped through me and was gone as quickly as it had risen. Time. The loss of it was the one motherfucking thing we both feared most.

She touched my face, her eyes questioning the truth of the matter, and I wanted to take the words back and eliminate them from my brain.

"I only mean that we need space to settle into our marriage before additional weight is added to our relationship. We'll have children. But first, I need to know I won't lose you."

"When we got married, Will, I made a commitment to you. You and me first. Always. Remember? We said we would choose each other first every single day." Elle kissed my mouth, the taste of salt from the tears lingering on her lips, then she presented me with a smile. "That doesn't mean you can't learn to share just a little."

"Maybe . . . but not today." The muscles in my face relaxed, and I grinned.

I slid my hand along the curve of her hip under the cover of my jacket, the silk of her gown all that separated our skin, and gripped her arse, using it to give her a slight lift until my mouth was on her neck. I sucked hard on the white birthmark located over her carotid, turning it a deep shade of red. Her pulse beat against my tongue when I licked it.

Mine, goddammit.

My clever wife, knowing that my cock was pushing above the waistband of my trousers, whispered in my ear. "Come to bed with me tonight. *Please.*"

And there it was in its richest form—her unquestionable power. I was desperate to shove into her tight, velvety heaven, but only a fool would believe the promise of sex could so easily influence a man like me. The power Elle wielded came from the way she needed me, the way she pleaded for me to give her what she needed. That she shamelessly wanted me was the force that crafted her power.

Maybe that was it—perhaps my desire for Elle to need me, for her to plead with me over it, was what made me the sick fuck I'd become.

I grabbed her hand and kissed the back of her fingers while contracting my glutes to redirect the blood away from my erection. The heaviness in my bollocks eased, but the ache for release persisted. "All right, baby," I breathed. "I won't leave you alone. I'll come to bed."

Sirens. Blaring sirens sounded, and flashing blue and red beams illuminated the vicinity.

Taylor stopped the car in the middle of the street.

The rotating blades of a helicopter thrummed above the stalled traffic.

"It's the Met Police's firearms command. There's been an attack at Kensington train station. Command is searching all passenger cars. We won't be permitted to pass." Taylor lowered his hand from his comms earpiece and cursed. "They pulled your brother out of the car ahead, sir."

26

The emergency lights of the Met Police armed response vehicles allowed me to see Thomas's silhouette. He was facing one of the vehicles with his hands flattened against it, his head dropped between his arms and his legs spread wide. They were searching him for weapons.

Neither of us was armed. We were no longer forced to assume that risk because Taylor and Evans could now carry legally, and one of them was always with Elle.

"What the fuck do they think they're doing?" I snarled. "Get your shoes on, Elle."

"Don't even," Ben said from the front passenger seat. "They want nothing more than for you to give them a reason to take you into custody, and you know it. You're not getting out of this goddamned car."

"Commissioner Brown would never do such a thing," Elle interjected.

Ben twisted to face her. "Not the commissioner. We know you've got him, and that's quite an advantage you've gained for us, but the home secretary has bribed foot soldiers on the ground and given direction to apprehend your husband should an opportunity arise." He turned to me. "They don't want Thomas. They pulled him out to get to you. Don't play into it."

During our last meeting, Director Martin mentioned that his superior, the home secretary, who was also the commissioner's director, was losing patience with the prime minister's recent deference to the Crown's rather discreet commands.

I made a mental note to visit to the prime minister soon to make certain he and the Crown and I continued to be on the same page. Our agreement provided protection for Elle and kept me out of prison. Most government leaders, like the home secretary, understood that I was one among a short list of killers who was permitted to walk free and prosper. I'd earned my place on the list by eliminating national security menaces as ordered by the Crown or the Security Service, before and after my father's passing, as well as by way of financial blackmail.

"They will give me no choice—they'll force me out of the car just the same. Identify yourself as an AFO, Taylor, and if they make her get out of the car, you cover every fucking centimeter of her body with your own. And Taylor, I want some goddamned names."

No one knew the politics of this city better than I did. The home secretary loathed me enough to allow this delay of firearms command resources during the chaotic aftermath of a terror attack, in which innocent people were frightened and injured or worse.

Panic was written all over Elle's face. She dug her fingers into my thigh and said nothing, her words locked inside the anxiety that consumed her. Rage beat through my veins as I watched her suffer through another hell she didn't deserve.

"Elle, stay in the car unless I tell you to step out. Don't listen to anyone else. It doesn't matter what they say. You will listen only to me." My voice was low, my tone hard-hitting. I wanted complete obedience from her in this instance, and behaving in a hawkish manner was the only way to get that from her, to make her understand the severity of the situation. "You'll look at me and agree."

"Okay," she breathed, her gaze sealed onto mine. "Only you."

"This isn't about us. We're in the wrong place at the wrong time, and that's unfortunate, but that's all it is. We must keep it that way. Yes?"

If she were physically exposed in such a volatile setting, it would be impossible for me to maintain my focus on getting us the hell out of there without rousing my anger.

She nodded. "Don't upset them, Will. Don't lose your temper and make it about us. Get back into the car with me as quickly as you can."

I bent to kiss her lips to reassure her of my compliance, and armed command officers wrenched open all four car doors.

"AFO," Taylor quickly shouted with his hands held high. "I'm an authorized firearms officer for the Met." He looked back at me. "Sir, put your hands above your head so my colleagues can see that you are no threat." Ben had already done the same.

"The three of us will step out of the car if that's your request. I insist you allow the Countess of Sussex to remain inside the vehicle and close the doors for her safety," he added.

The home secretary—the smug prick who directed the armed response unit—wanted me, not Elle. He considered her an innocent party regarding my crimes, and his foot soldiers seemed to understand that. Thank Christ. This had been the most significant reason for me choosing to reclaim my grandfather's title, to give it to Elle. Not only because she deserved respect but because she could more easily be identified in precarious situations where it may save her from harm.

"Countess, you may remain in the vehicle. The rest of you, get the fuck out, and keep your hands above your heads," one of the command officers said. He was armed with a Sig Sauer semiautomatic rifle.

The temperature of my blood rapidly increased.

The three of us stepped out of the car while Elle slid across the leather upholstery to my side of the car. I held her gaze, warning her to do as she'd been told. She gave a small nod to reassure me that she would follow my instructions, and in turn, she narrowed her eyes to caution me about my next moves.

Reproving messages echoed inside my head.

Keep your shit together. Rein in the anger to keep her safe.

I spread my hands flat on the roof of the car and kept my mouth shut when I was forced against it and ordered to spread my legs. I would not risk being taken away from Elle.

Thomas's form appeared in the headlights as he made his way to my side. "You're wasting the people's resources here," he said to the officers. "There is a terrorist fucking off round the city somewhere, but instead of tracking him, you choose to harass an uninvolved citizen and his family?"

"Thomas," I growled. "Go back to your car."

I didn't need my cocky brother provoking anyone into unnecessary action, least of all me.

"You know why. Go. Now." I angled my head in his direction and nailed him with my stare. He needed to see the intensity of the anger rising in me. He would understand, and he would go back to his car and wait for us.

Thomas returned a knowing look and took a couple of steps backwards. "Move this along, then, brother, and let's get the hell out of here."

I said nothing, dropped my head between my arms, and submitted to the body search.

Another of the command officers stepped into my space, leaning in close. "Tell me, why does the *Earl of Sussex* choose to spend so much time in London?"

Breath stormed in and out of my nostrils, and my hands started to itch. Red. It was everywhere. I shut my eyes tightly for a minute and flexed my fingers against the metal of the car. "You know why, motherfucker. You know who I am." Low and steady. A restrained warning.

Elle rested her fingertips against the window glass near my face. Her pleading eyes burned into mine. "I love you," she mouthed.

I couldn't say it back, not in the state of mind I was in. I wouldn't soil words meant to express how I loved her by saying them when rage consumed me, so I dropped my eyes. "Get on with it, you corrupt son of a bitch," I snarled.

He followed protocol and searched me as he was trained to do, but before he removed his hands from my body, he stepped even closer to hide the way he ran his riot baton between my legs and pressed it against my testicles.

"Devon Parker is a friend of mine. We couldn't have predicted this opportunity, but I'm quite sure he won't mind me delivering his regards to your pretty wife a day earlier than planned," he said.

He was not only paid well by the home secretary, but also he had a personal connection.

And with that, he'd marked his own death.

BEAUTIFUL WHITE LIES

From: Ellie <ellie.hastings@hastingsgroup.co.uk>
To: Isobel <isobel.james@hastingsgroup.co.uk>

It's been a while. There hasn't been much time for me to spend alone with my thoughts, so I need you to hear me, Isobel.

Will is falling back into the shadows that haunt his soul. I saw it in his eyes last night. A menacing combination of emotions stirs inside of him.

The years he had with his father trouble him more now than ever, though he doesn't share the details with me. It's not difficult to see that Richard Hastings abused his power and his sons. Will promised we would talk about it one day, and I know that he will keep his word.

And now, enemies we thought were gone are finding their way back into our life through others left behind. My husband will eliminate these threats. I know him. I know this.

He'd said after Connecticut that he would take no more lives. I don't fault him for the lie.

White lies. The untruths we tell and the secrets we keep from our loved ones to hold them safe from harm, to spare them emotional pain. Everyone lies. Everyone who loves tells white lies. Some are little, some are not.

We tell them knowing the truth will ultimately come to light. We convince ourselves that we can hold them close, never let them go. But we know the deception will be revealed in good time. It rips our hearts to pieces when we tell these lies. Still, we tell the lies.

You lied to keep me safe and again to keep Lissie safe. Your intent was good. I can see the beauty of it now. Your deceit gave us Will. He's everything Lissie needs. His soul is the only thing that can free me. He is everything I've waited for, the one person I can't live without.

From the moment Will and I returned to England after he'd been shot, he has been committed to finding the power to control his anger, to harnessing its influence in order to change his legacy. He has done well, but my own efforts have set him back.

I thought protecting him from Ethan's obscurity would spare him the pain.

I was wrong.

My secrecy only hurt him more.

27

Mrs. Bates stood near our bed and spoke low in her rolling Irish lilt. "Thomas and the other lads are waiting in the kitchen. He says you must get up, that you and the countess have important plans this morning."

We'd arrived home soon after the Met's armed command had finished searching our car. I feared the man who'd patted me down had no idea with whom he was fucking and what kind of enemy he had created for himself. One day he would face the consequence of being Devon Parker's messenger.

I had carried my exhausted wife from the car to our bedroom. She'd fallen asleep straightaway with the side of her face resting on the center of my chest, her long locks of hair blanketing parts of us both. I had monitored her breathing, bracing for the nightmares.

I hadn't been able to sleep. The urge to quietly slip out into the night and track down that motherfucker who dared to place his baton between my legs and deliver that message to Elle had been strong.

The number of faces that inhabited the worst part of me would soon increase.

Anger had punched me in the gut, reminding me who I was born to be, showing me that my father's purpose for me would never change, no matter how I strived to be a different man. It was a madness. It had encouraged me to leave Elle alone in our bed for the hunt, to make another kill to secure her future.

Still. Nothing was stronger than my determination to shelter my angel inside my arms when she was distraught, so I had stayed. She had been panic-stricken, though she'd tried to hide it.

My mind had finally shut down at the break of dawn, and I had fallen asleep after pulling Elle's backside tightly against my body. She had rolled from my chest onto her side. That was her tell when she found peaceful rest, a sign that she was clear of the nightmares.

Mrs. Bates tidied the bedside table and waited for my response.

I pulled the sheet above my waist quickly as if she had never seen my naked body. Our housekeeper was a fixture in our homes, caring for my wife as if it were her life's work, so it was sometimes unavoidable. She was entirely focused on her tasks and didn't seem to notice, and if she did, she didn't let it show. I supposed she knew before taking us on that there would be nudity in our bedroom given it was the only place we could find peace from the rest of the world.

Elle and I had accepted that a sense of danger and urgency would often take over parts of our life together. Our peace was limited to small fragments of time in between.

"He's quite right, Mrs. Bates. What time is it?" I covered my eyes as she opened the draperies, letting the frequently scarce sunshine beat against the windowpanes to wake Elle.

"It's quarter to nine."

"Christ." I sat up. "I'll ring Sean and have the commissioner sent here."

"I brought breakfast up with me, dearest," she said to Elle, handing me my mobile from the table. "Let me fetch the tray from the landing so you can get started on coffee and toast."

"I don't want to get up," Elle grumbled. She hadn't bothered to open her eyes.

"We're due to see Commissioner Brown at ten o'clock, baby." Her pretty arse was there next to my hand, mine for the taking. I watched Mrs. Bates exit the room and slid my hand along the curve of it.

Elle complained about the appointment and pushed back into my hand for a firmer touch.

No time, goddammit.

By the time I found some pajama bottoms and came back from the toilet, Elle was sitting up in bed, knees pulled to her chest beneath the sheet, sipping on coffee. There was a smear of raspberry jam near the corner of her mouth. Her hair was a wild mess.

She is so beautiful. Need her.

She smiled. "Stop staring and come eat these fried eggs she carried up for you."

On my hands and knees, I prowled from the foot of the bed to get to her. "Come here. . . . There's something on your face. . . ."

Her face lifted to mine. I feigned wiping away the jam with my thumb but then licked the red sweetness off of her face.

"It's quite good. Give me more."

Elle set her coffee aside on the bedside table and dipped her finger into the pot. She painted her bottom lip with the jam, and I sucked it off.

"More," I ordered.

When she pulled her forefinger out of the pot again, she hesitated, holding it upright without touching anything. "Tell me, Will, where do you want it this time?" Her voice had taken on a sensual huskiness, and she hit me with a shy smile. She was turned on.

"Let me show you what I want." I pulled the sheet away from

her bare body and gaped for a minute before dragging her jam-covered finger from her neck to her pebbled nipple, circling it, making it even harder. She gasped and arched her back. Christ, she was touching herself, and it was so beautiful to watch. When I lifted her finger from her breast, she groaned.

"More. Please, Will. More."

I smirked and grabbed the jam pot. "Yes, baby, I'm quite hungry. I need more."

She curved two fingers and scooped more jam from the jar. I placed those fingertips on her other nipple and watched her circle it and arch again, then I dragged her two fingers down along her abdomen and pressed them to her clit. She cried out.

"Don't come, Elle. Not without me." I pushed back and settled my weight on my heels and watched her work the berry jam round her sweet little button. I stroked my throbbing cock while I watched her pant and writhe in pleasure before I stopped her. "Grip the pillow above your head."

She resisted. "Will . . . I need . . ."

I grabbed her wrists. "You will do as you're told, angel, or you'll get nothing at all."

Her eyes went wide, she swallowed hard, and she submitted to me with a nod.

I was demanding more of her in bed as she'd asked, acknowledging that she was indeed not breakable, though I had never looked at her that way. Strength and will is what I saw whenever I looked at my wife. If she needed me to prove it to her, then I would, but my way. I would never smack her arse again.

"Good girl," I murmured against her skin, my mouth devouring the fruit on her stomach. I drew my tongue upwards along the raspberry-red stroke she'd painted for me until I reached her hardened nipples. I sucked them both, drawing each tightly between my teeth and pulling for a few seconds before releasing them to give her the sharp sensation of erotic pain.

She writhed and moaned each time, arching into the slight sting. "Oh God," she cried.

"There is no god, angel. There's only me. And you are mine." I placed tender kisses on her nipples and blew to change the sensation to one without the promise of pain.

"You are my god," she breathed as I dragged my mouth to her neck.

Her words made my erection kick out against her stomach and my heart pound faster in my chest. I loved her beyond words. I was obsessed with her. Nothing else mattered. There was nothing else because she was everything. And I was hers.

"I need you, Will. Please don't let rage split us up again. I can't survive without you."

I lifted my head and met her eyes. She knew. She'd seen it the night before when I had looked into the car window, when she'd pressed her hand to the glass and said she loved me.

"Never, Elle. I promise. Just help me keep it straight."

She brought her hands down to my face. "We can beat it."

Then I kissed her, shoving past her lips with my tongue and taking her mouth with such brutal force that she pushed my face back. "I'm sorry," I breathed and then kissed her again with as much tenderness as I could gather.

I was fucking desperate to be inside of her, for her to heal me.

"I'm going to make you come hard, Elle. Are you ready?"

"Yes. You'll fuck the hell out of me?" She grinned.

I couldn't help but grin as well as I pressed my cock against her body. Christ. "I'm quite a lot bigger than you, baby. Are you sure that's what you want?"

"Oh, yes. I want you to do it hard. And fast. From behind."

Another tender kiss on her lips. "If that's what you want, you know the rules—hands back to the pillow. Need to get you ready first, to take all of me. I do believe you left some of my breakfast between your legs."

28

Commissioner Brown held out his coffee mug for Mrs. Bates to refill, and I pushed my fingers through my damp hair. Elle was just making her way down the staircase. I'd asked her to take her time showering so that I might first have a few minutes alone with the commissioner. It wasn't about keeping secrets or withholding information. Anything he gave me I would share with her. I wanted to be sure he wasn't reserved in his responses to my questions for the sake of maintaining respect for my wife. Elle got that. She didn't like it, but she understood.

She and Thomas passed through the arched opening into the drawing room together. Mrs. Bates slid the pocket doors shut behind herself after handing Elle a glass of water.

The commissioner stood and greeted Elle. It was the first time I'd seen them together, and my call to separate him from her had been spot-on. His gaze held her with paternal affection. He would have been less frank to spare her further suffering, as a father or uncle or even a brother might do.

He would soften his words now that she was with us, but I couldn't. She needed to grasp the severity of what we were coming up against, and I needed her to experience the anxiety it would trigger while she was in my presence rather than have her hide it from me. I extended my hand to her.

"So, Commissioner, Devon Parker goes to trial soon, and you believe his conviction is a foregone conclusion based on Interpol's supporting evidence," I reiterated from our conversation. "Trafficking in automatic weapons by way of Eastern Europe will get him how many years in prison?"

"Seven to ten is the recommended sentence for a British citizen, but perhaps more in this case."

"For seven to ten years, perhaps more, as you say, he will sit behind bars with the ability to send his accomplices to threaten my wife—some of whom work for you. And I'm supposed to do what . . . ignore the risks? Hope none of his followers are fucked-up enough to hurt her before he gets out and tries to do it himself? Fuck if I will."

"No, we're not doing that, brother," Thomas said. "The commissioner understands what is at stake here and to what lengths you and I will go to keep Ellie safe."

Commissioner Brown took his seat and contemplated his next words for a minute. He looked at Elle, and she flashed a warm smile back at him. She liked him, trusted him even.

"I assure you the corrupt officer you encountered last night will be held to account. My advice is for you to work more closely with Director Martin on this case. As you know, his team is granted protection against criminal and rogue acts. I would not be granted the same."

MI5 relied on its agents and informers to provide intelligence for investigations into terrorism and espionage, so it operated differently than the nation's civil law enforcement agencies. Agents acting on behalf of the security service were permitted by the government to carry out criminal activity. Activism associated with the Order had been declared terrorism by the Crown.

I nodded, picked up my coffee, and pulled it close to my

mouth, speaking over the steam. "Thomas and I will work with the director. You will continue to counsel my wife on the matter. However, she may not see Parker again." I sipped while moving my gaze to hers. She dropped her eyes to her hands and twisted her wedding band round her finger.

Her name fell softly from my lips, and I took her hands into one of mine, placing them on my thigh, holding hers there beneath mine. When she lifted her gaze, I pitched her a small smile. The regret in her eyes cleared, and her lips curved, syncing with mine. We released a breath together.

No one said a word. The commissioner and Thomas each signaled their compliance to my command by bobbing their heads in agreement.

Elle leaned forward with more confidence, her leg rubbing against mine. "Is the video footage ready, Thomas? I'd like to take a look now." She turned back to me. "And then I want to go home. You can send for Sean or James Jackson or your investigator or whoever you need to work with from Eastridge—I don't care. But I want to go just as soon as we see this video."

My angel had had enough. Her anxiety was on high alert, and she needed the comfort of our family home. She needed to hold Lissie tightly in her arms.

"Of course, baby. You're right. Let's get out of this goddamned city for a while."

"Come with me, Ellie," Thomas said, curving his fingers to indicate that she go to him. "Will can wrap up here while you and I fire up the footage on the monitor in the library."

Elle kissed my cheek, presented her hand to the commissioner when he gestured for it, and then hooked her arm through my brother's. As they walked away, I watched the sway of her hips. I recalled how she looked, smelled, and sounded as she screamed my name when I made her come on all fours only an hour before. She had been so lovely. So bloody fucking lovely.

Commissioner Brown cleared his throat.

That shit always pissed me off—the throat clearing to get my attention.

"You know how this is going to go down, commissioner," I started. "You will notify Martin of the sentencing and correctional facility transport details, and in that short window of time during his transfer, Devon Parker will die. I don't see another option at this point. Do you?"

He shook his head and hardened his blue gaze, locking it onto mine. "I've spent time with Devon Parker. He has a sick mind, Hastings. If he is presented with an opportunity to avenge Simon, he will hurt her first, and then he will murder her. He has priors. He's hurt other women, but he will kill your wife. So no, I can't see another way in this instance. We must cut the head off the bloody snake."

"And I'm sorry, mate," the commissioner added. "I haven't had an opportunity since Ethan's passing to deliver my personal condolences. Ethan and I were never close, but nonetheless, he was a friend. He was happy for you, you know."

"Thank you. He gave his life for hers, for me." I dropped my chin, rubbed my eyes.

He lied to me about so many things. Not sure I care that he did.

Losing my older brother still hurt. He had been my confidant, my business partner. He had covered for me whenever I'd fallen into a binge with whatever suited my addiction-inclined tendencies, though nothing and no one satisfied me back then.

Ethan had been smaller than Thomas and I, with less physical strength, and he'd known our father had undervalued him because of it. But Ethan had never quit a fight, no matter how hard he'd been pushed or how many times one of us had broken his damn arm or his nose. He'd been an excellent marksman from an early age, but that had never been enough for our father. His sons had to be warriors. At some point when we were in our late teens, I took on Ethan's fights, and our father repurposed him for rebuilding the family's financial holdings.

My older brother had been all about the money, all right, and he'd been quite good at networking and sourcing. He'd had a genuine talent for pulling in business opportunities and setting us up with an advantage. But ultimately, he somehow had fucked up negotiations in the deals he'd attempted to close on his own. I became the moneymaker, closing deals that made us billions. . . . And my father hadn't lived long enough to get his hands on a goddamned penny or see the irony of it all.

"Listen. I'm not certain Elle's sighting of Parker last night wasn't a manifestation of the anxiety disorder she suffers from. To be clear, Commissioner, I want this incident kept quiet."

The commissioner extended his hand, and we shook in silent agreement.

I walked him to the door, pleased with our understandings, and headed for the library to join my brother and my wife. It was quite a relief to have an ally in the city who cared about saving Elle's life without the expectation that I would deliver a hit or lend my financial influence in return. I released a heavy breath. Devon Parker was mine—his ghost belonged to me.

Elle's face was pained with worry and confusion. She was on her feet, staring at the large monitor on the wall with the remote in her hand. Rewind. Play. Rewind. Play. She played the segment of video footage over and over.

"I'm not crazy," she whispered.

"You're done with this, Elle. Something scared the hell out of you last night, but it wasn't captured on camera, that's all. And now we know it wasn't Devon Parker." I pried the small silver remote from her fingers and tossed it to Thomas. "Unmanned video surveillance never captures what it should in large settings like that one."

"I inspected the camera locations myself, Ellie. None were positioned in a way that would reproduce the view from where you were standing. It's a technical issue. The security system install was done poorly. You can't beat yourself up over it," Thomas added.

Elle nodded and the anguish marking her expression eased. "Okay," she breathed. "Okay. It's not easy when I can't put my own eyes on him in his jail cell, but you're both certain he was and is still there, so I'll deal." Her eyes met mine, and I pulled her close. "I trust you, Will."

"Devon Parker can't get to you. I swear to that," Thomas said.

She locked her arms round my waist and rested her cheek against my chest, her head positioned so she could make eye contact with Thomas. "I trust you both."

Was that pain in his eyes? The suffering in his eyes was different right then, if only for a heartbeat, but I recognized it. It was the kind of pain that split my chest wide when I was unable to soothe her, and the idea that he might be feeling that sentiment stirred the bloodthirst that lived in me.

My brother moved away abruptly to cut the video feed. He knew I'd caught his pained expression. "You two should head home to Eastridge. I'll remain in the city tonight so we have eyes on the situation from this angle. It'll be more advantageous for one of us to be here."

"You'll need to drive home for the partnership meeting. I want to keep the business plan on track. Sean will make arrangements for the others to attend via Skype or whatever the hell it is he uses, and he'll come along with me to the estate. The secretary he's been training will cover his desk at the office."

Christ. One night wasn't enough time to put distance between myself and what I'd just witnessed in my brother's eyes. I gnashed my back teeth together, causing tension in my jaws.

"Ellie's private secretary?"

"Yes. Spend time with Ms. Smith while Sean is out. Task her with confidential matters. Review her background information. Make sure nothing was missed." I pressed Elle's ear harder against the center of my chest and covered the other one. A stupid fucking instinct to protect her beautiful, pure light.

She pushed at my hand. She could still hear me, of course, and she would reprimand me for my behavior as soon as she escaped my hold.

Let her scold me. It'll give me an opportunity to shut that sweet little mouth with mine and reclaim her.

The thought of tasting her caused my cock to rise. My lips twitched.

"Do not fuck my wife's secretary, Thomas," I ordered before releasing Elle.

29

Two hours later, our bags were packed, and we were headed south towards East Sussex county. Mrs. Bates hadn't wanted to delay her own return by waiting for her brother to pick her up, so she rode shotgun in the front with Taylor in the Bentley. It worked out well enough for Elle. Recognizing that I would be tied up with business calls, she intended to use the drive time to review household matters with Mrs. Bates before we arrived at Eastridge.

The grand country estate once owned by my father and several of my grandfathers now belonged to me. As my wife, Elle outranked my mother and was hurled into a role in which she was leaned upon for her preferences and decisions in the running of both houses. She quite disliked the tediousness of it all, but she was settling into it, innovating new family rituals and carefully preserving some of the old traditions—sometimes reshaping them to better suit our current needs while making it more palatable for future generations.

"We need to prepare rooms for Sean and James," I heard her tell Mrs. Bates. "I'd like to keep them away from the girls and

Mary. Will may keep late working hours, and we don't want the family disturbed." She turned to me. "When is James arriving?"

I cut out of my phone conversation with the investigator for a minute. The retired intelligence officer was surveilling the men expected to rouse the Order and looking for Sarah Parker. I'd added another assignment—monitoring activity at the Met's central custody facility where Devon Parker was imprisoned.

"Late. Not until after dinner."

She stroked my arm and continued with her planning session, and I smirked. Her confidence was already soaring. Being home on the southeast coast of England affected my wife that way. It changed her in a profound manner. She became assertive once her strength was unchained from the apprehensive state she dwelled in each time we remained in London for more than a few days.

Someday she won't have to spend much time there.

Hastings Group was doing quite well again. Ethan and I had built a wildly successful private equity company, but we had taken some heavy hits when I stayed in the States before bringing Elle back, and again after Ethan's death. Thomas and I had been clever enough as a team to quickly recover the financial losses and recapture the firm's aggressive momentum. It was time to give Thomas his professional due and make him a full partner. But that was only half of the equation necessary for me to reduce the amount of time I spent inside HG's operations.

We planned to bring two additional partners into the firm. It would take four active managing partners for me to be afforded the type of business schedule I wanted. A schedule that allowed for Elle to join me in most cases or offered us the opportunity to bow out completely. Opening up the firm to more associates was never something Ethan and I had considered, but each time I looked at the woman now at my side, it became clear that I had to surrender the egocentric footing with which my older brother and I had founded the company.

James Jackson had earned his position as partner. Christ, he'd held shit together time and again when I did not. After James was invested as a managing partner and the three of us discovered our fourth, Thomas would be able to breathe easier. He was under a great deal of pressure to pull his weight straightaway, but not only that, he also covered for me when I became preoccupied with my wife. And when some of the burden was lifted from my brother's shoulders, when he was successfully executing contracts on his own, I could become the CEO who rolled into the city for short periods to close significant deals and drink Scotch with investors and foundation donors.

In the beginning, it had all been for Elle, and in the very end, it will still be for her. Building a moneymaking enterprise had been about accumulating wealth for Ethan, but for me, it was the means to how and when I would finally have her. It was how I channeled my obsession, how I prepared my life for the day I would possess her. Money was power, and power was necessary for me to have her and to keep her alive.

My obsession changed the moment I touched her hand on that pier in Stonington for the first time. Truth be told, an obsession never fails, never ceases, but mine did change. The longing and fixation had always been about me, about what I wanted to take from her.

Jesus Christ, how I wanted to own every part of her.

But when I finally had the chance to feel her pain, kiss her lips, see her dreams, and hear her laugh, I fell in love with her the right way. I fell for her heart . . . her soul . . . her mind. I was no longer in love with my father's plan for me to save her and keep her as my prize, no longer in love with the desire to win what was supposed to be mine. My obsession transformed then, and it became an addiction to the deep, mutual connection Elle and I had discovered between us. Not another goddamned thing mattered to me if it wasn't something she needed or demanded of me.

My heart had traded one sickness for another.

"Yes, I'm still here," I said into the phone to the investigator. "What about Sarah Parker? Where are we with that case?"

"Well, Devon Parker wasn't lying when he told your wife he assumed she was dead. In late July of last year, his mother was granted a declaration of presumed death. The court document indicates that no living family member had seen her alive in the prior seven years. At the time of the filing, the family members who legally attested to *in absentia* were the mother, Simon Parker, and Devon Parker."

"Was there an application for an inquest without a body?"

"Yes, the Kent County Coroner applied to the Secretary of State's office for one," he said.

"What about a police report? The government can't issue a registration of presumed death without a legitimate enquiry."

"Quite right. It couldn't have been certified without one. The police examination was handled by the Tonbridge Police Department. The report cites no precise evidence, but the assigned detective indicated in his statement that Sarah Parker was a known drug abuser and that he believed she was dead."

"Is the mother still living in Tonbridge?" I put the call on speaker so Elle could listen. Her stare was burning into the side of my face, and she'd gone quiet.

"She is. I've been to Mrs. Parker's home twice, but she won't agree to speak with me or even fully open the door. From what I could see, she's rather frail."

"How certain are you that she lives alone and that there are no other children? Sons, daughters, grandchildren."

"She receives a government attendance allowance and universal credit for housing. A nurse visits once a day. I believe the woman is terminally ill. No one else enters or leaves the flat. Devon Parker is her only living relative."

Christ. Elle would insist on seeing the old woman herself.

As if she'd read my mind, Elle jumped into the conversation.

"We need to go see her, Will. She's the only person who can confirm this and give us the reason behind it all. And if she's hurting, if her sons have neglected her over the years . . . she's Lissie's biological grandmother, and I need . . . I don't know. I want her to be okay. Maybe she'll talk to me if I'm alone."

I would have expected nothing less from my wife. I hated the idea of her doing it alone, but I wouldn't forbid her from contributing to the investigation. We'd made an agreement to share and work together, and I was determined to keep my end of the bargain.

"We'll see her together," I said. "It sounds as if she's in financial distress in addition to her physical suffering, and I'd like to help."

The woman's losses were on me. My father took her husband. I had seen to the death of her oldest son, Simon Parker. And soon I would take Devon's life as well. I couldn't help but think of my own mother and what her life might have become had she lost us all. I owed Mrs. Parker recompense—some comfort to see her through to the end of her impoverished life.

"Text me the address of the flat and the visiting nurse's schedule. Focus on surveilling her son," I told the private investigator before disconnecting our call.

My wife slipped her fingers beneath the cuff of my sleeve. Her soft touch on the inside of my wrists was a gift that I craved. "You are a good man, William Hastings."

"Mrs. Parker doesn't deserve to be punished for the sins of her husband and her sons any more than my mother should have to pay for my father's and mine. If she accepts our help, I will provide complete financial support for her. But Elle, that's as far as it goes. There is no room for the old woman in our daughter's life."

Elle stretched to kiss me on the lips. She locked her eyes into mine and nodded. "We need to think about what we'll tell Lissie in the future. Right now? I can't see telling her or anyone else outside of our small circle that she's not Isobel's biological daughter. I can't break her little heart with another loss."

I caressed her bottom lip with my thumb. "You love her so beautifully. We should tell her soon about Ethan. It'll provide her with a greater sense of belonging to know that she's a Hastings in name and blood."

"Let's wait until we resolve this mess with the Parkers, Will. Please. It will change her. She will ask why the lies were told. I need more time. I want to give her the truth she deserves."

Soon after we first met, when I had confined her under my protection in the beach cottage she owned, Elle expressed how afraid she was to be Lissie's legal guardian. She was lost then, naïve and unaware of her own truths, but not any longer. Somewhere along the way, my wife found her fortitude, her desires, herself. She became the woman who loved and gave forgiveness and gifted everyone round her with something special, something untouchable. Elle was the perfect mother for Lissie, and she would be for our children as well.

"Okay. When you're ready," I breathed, my words touching her lips first before I kissed them. "We'll get this right, Elle. All of it, I promise. And you'll have everything you've asked me for."

She pulled a sharp inhale through her mouth. "You're talking about our own children—is that what you mean?"

I didn't say anything. The words stuck on my tongue, so she broke the silence.

"I know it's hard for you to talk about it. But you're trying. . . . I can see that. And Will, I appreciate that you're taking an honest look, sizing it up to see how it might feel." The secret smile. It changed me a little more each time she shared it.

I lifted one shoulder into a blasé shrug. "Just want you to know."

"I do," she whispered.

The text message with Mrs. Parker's address buzzed my mobile.

Tonbridge was ten miles ahead. We usually bypassed the old town without as much as a thought, but it was now one more portentous obstruction I had to eliminate from our path.

I displayed the message for Elle. "Shall we make the stop today?"

WALKING AMONG GHOSTS

From: Ellie <ellie.hastings@hastingsgroup.co.uk>
To: Isobel <isobel.james@hastingsgroup.co.uk>

You're gone from my dreams. Vanished completely, Isobel.

Even though you're no longer here, and your spirit no longer visits my sleeping mind, the number of lies you left behind continues to increase, one building on top of another. I wish we could have been partners, that you would have confided in me.

Maybe you believed I wasn't strong enough.

But I am, and I hope you can see that now from wherever you are.

We found Mrs. Parker. She is kind and warm.

She was hesitant before receiving us at her rundown old flat. God, the smell. I made her some tea using an old saucepan, and we brought in Mrs. Bates to assess the living conditions and help to convince Mrs. Parker to allow us to move her into a comfortable residential nursing facility in London, where she would have a private suite with around-the-clock nursing staff and palliative care.

She is dying alone. Metastatic breast cancer.

Even if Will allowed Devon Parker to live, the hateful man would not take care of his mother.

I can't wrap my head around the fact that the Parker children chose to abandon their lovely mother. She has been left penniless for God knows how long.

It all started with one lie that has affected so many. I often wonder why you and Gran carried the story forward after my parents were gone. It would have been so easy to share the secret, and we three could have lived together in the truth of my family's real identity.

But here I stand, living in the aftermath among the ghosts—living with your ghost—watching an innocent woman suffer alone through the end of her life.

I know it's not as simple as sharing a single secret. I do. Because our fathers compounded the original lie by using it to cover their missteps and sate their egos. But maybe there would have been fewer ghosts.

Will tells me I'm wrong about that. There would be one more ghost, not fewer, he insists—and that one more would be mine. Without the lies, as much as we hate them, he believes I would have been found sooner and my life taken.

Once we had Mrs. Parker's permission, Will arranged for her to be housed and cared for in London, where we can keep tabs on her without interference from Tonbridge locals. We have no plans to introduce her to Lissie, and for now, we have no plans to tell our little girl that you are not her biological mother.

Sarah Parker is dead. What good would come from telling Lissie that she had another maternal link . . . another connection that failed her . . . another person gone from her life forever?

But in order to keep this information to ourselves, we must be careful not to reveal who your father was.

30

Elle insisted she would walk into the house on her own when we arrived at Eastridge, though she was quite weak. I called my mother as we approached the ridge and ordered her to find Jessica and otherwise keep our arrival quiet until we figured out what was happening. I didn't want Lissie unnerved by Elle's unexpected condition.

We had stopped for lunch at a small diner outside of Tonbridge after settling things with Mrs. Parker. Elle later into the drive complained of a headache and mild nausea. We'd assumed the soup or banoffee pie she'd eaten was bad—but just a few miles from home, an unusual fatigue had settled over her, and I could see anxiety chipping away at her resolve.

The fact that the Parker family was still hurting her made my fucking blood boil.

Mrs. Bates had been the one to persuade the frail old woman to accept our offer of financial responsibility for housing and medical care. Mrs. Parker plainly hadn't trusted me. She'd taken quite well to my wife but couldn't bring herself to make eye contact with me. Her lack of confidence was to be expected. Her family's blood dripped from my hands.

Elle had warned that my size was intimidating Mrs. Parker and had asked me to stay seated while she and Mrs. Bates had moved about the flat to pack up what little the woman owned. I'd gone out to the car instead and continued working over the phone with my lawyer to get a private room secured at a nursing home in London. It hadn't been difficult to circumvent the waiting list. I had authorized a generous donation to the institution's operating fund through one of HG's private real estate subsidiaries.

Money talks and all that bullshit.

I kept my arm round Elle's waist as we made our way from the car but lifted her into my arms once we were inside the house and carried her upstairs to our master suite. She rested her head on my shoulder, finally giving in to the fatigue wrecking her body. The scent of her hair drifted into my face.

For a fleeting moment, I saw a vision of my wife dragging her toes through sand along some tropical coastline, plucking little white shells from the shallow water.

"I'm fine, Will," she said. "I need a nap, that's all. It's been a long week. God, I'm so happy to be home."

"Are you lying to me again, baby? Because last time I checked, that wasn't true—napping in the middle of the day has never been your thing." I kissed her forehead to soften the accusation.

Tears glistened in her eyes, but she didn't look away. She met my gaze with defiance.

There's my angel. Come on, challenge me. Challenge the anxiety.

"Yes, Elle, this week was rough, and you soldiered through it. You were strong even when you should have leaned on me." I set my wife on her feet outside the doors of our suite, and as if I needed to further demonstrate my stamina, I pounded on my chest. "Here is our physical strength. My body is made to handle the effects of our stress. Yours is not. I won't allow you to become broken this way."

Her lips were pressed into a tight line, and her eyes still burned with a rebellious spark.

Good. Come on.

Stubborn determination was part of her process. But it would soften, and she would hear me. Feel me.

"What would you have me do differently, Will?"

"You tell me. It's quite clear you're holding out on me, suppressing emotion."

The softness came then, faster than expected. "If we could get away from it all . . ." she whispered. Her lids dropped. "I need to be alone with you for more than a few hours here and there." She opened them and lifted her lovely green eyes back to mine. "We need some time alone. No family, no staff. Just us."

"We're on the same page, Elle. You know I couldn't agree more. You've never said the words, never demanded it of me. And I have to ask, why are you telling me this now?"

She shrugged. "It's time."

"Time?" I reached behind her and placed my hand over the electronic door sensor on the wall. The door opened, and I forced her backwards one step at a time until we were beyond the threshold. I closed us in. "Explain."

"I want the honeymoon you promised."

Elle staggered, the fatigue causing her movements to become awkward, and I caught her. I pulled her into my arms. "Do you?"

"Yes, I do. It was always important to me. From the moment you made the promise, I wanted it. Do you remember what you promised—on the beach at Lords Point?"

"Yes, of course. I never forget my pledges to you."

"I know this sounds selfish, but I want to not care about what everyone else needs for just a little while. So, I'm saying it now, Will. When we leave this house again, I'd like for us to go to Paris. Alone."

A strand of hair fell onto her cheek, and I tucked it behind her ear. "I'd like that as well. Paris it is, baby."

She smiled. Adoration. The affection I craved. "I need to lie down and recover my strength, but I'll be totally refreshed by dinner. You should go see Lissie. She must be home from school by now."

I kissed her lips. Four times. Or was it five? "I'll send in Jessica when I go. Mother called her back from the children's clinic, and she's waiting to see you. You must let her help you feel better."

"I do feel better. I'm sure those sick children need her nursing skills more than I do, but all right."

"Promise me you won't hide what you're feeling, that you'll tell me what you need. Nothing is more important to me, Elle, than what you feel, what you need. Don't shut me out."

She nodded. "Lie down with me for a minute before you go?"

"Are you well enough for me to draw you a hot bath?"

A sweet smile curved her lips, and she hugged my neck. "Yes. That sounds amazing."

"Done." I kissed the top of her head, then pulled her into our bathroom.

She waited on the armchair near the tub while I filled it and dropped in some of her favorite rose oil. I undressed my wife and loved her graceful, feminine body with my eyes, dragging my stare from those sensual lips to the curve of her arse to her toes and back to her mesmerizing green eyes. I kissed her mouth, her neck, her shoulders.

"You are strong, but you are also perfectly delicate, my angel. You will not deny me that part of you," I said close to her ear. "You are mine."

Goose bumps covered her soft creamy flesh, and my cock reached out for her. I held both of her hands as she stepped into the steaming, fragrant bath.

I turned to go, and another thought circled through my mind.

Pivoting to see her eyes, I asked, "The pregnancy test was negative?"

"It was. You read it yourself."

I nodded and left her alone in that rose-scented water to contemplate whatever the lie was that she clearly still safe-guarded.

31

The next morning, after breakfast was finished and I'd had a walk about the south garden overlooking the English Channel with Elle, Lissie, and the four pups, I hit the war room to join Thomas, James Jackson, and my executive assistant, Sean.

Christ, springtime had arrived out of nowhere, and Lissie would soon turn eight. We'd told her about our impending visit to Paris, and all she wanted for her birthday right then was to come along with us to France. She had negotiated her way to victory in true Hastings form, emerging from the deal with a trip to the Continent later in the year over the summer holiday.

How do I say We're going to Paris *in French?* Lissie had asked.

Nous allons à Paris. Repeat it back to me.

I wanted her to become fluent early. The education system didn't place much emphasis on foreign-language learning. The curriculum provided wasn't offered until kids were eleven or twelve years old. But my mother was an excellent teacher, and she'd started French lessons with Lissie not long after our arrival from the States.

Nous allons à Paris, my two beauties had chanted with their hands linked, giggling, twirling round and round through the wild primroses and tall grass, the pups chasing at their heels.

Sean jumped up from his seat at the conference table and poured me a cup of coffee when I entered the war room. "We're ready, sir. Thomas has the lawyers on standby for the video conference, and printed copies of the contracts are here on the table."

I took a drink. "Thank you. Before we get to the video con, I want to quickly discuss accommodations for Paris. Extend the apartment lease you secured. In fact, leave it open-ended for now."

"I'll contact the real estate broker after this meeting and negotiate a flexible agreement. How long do you estimate staying on?"

"We'll stay for as long as Elle is happy to be in France. Be prepared for additional fees for changing the terms and rewriting the contract without a prearranged limit. Make it happen, Sean, and don't let the broker fuck you over."

Thomas disconnected a phone call. He'd arrived after breakfast. "That wasn't the plan. What is this about?"

"Don't read into it, brother. My wife wants an extended holiday in Paris, that is all. I have no intention to cap the time as long as she wants to be there. When she and I leave here next week, we're going to the Continent straightaway."

"What? Christ. Well, you could have mentioned it sooner. We need to put together a revised security plan and prepare the team."

I nodded for the sake of saving face in that moment. Thomas would be disagreeable when he learned Elle and I were going to France alone. It would be a heated discussion, and it needed to be held in private. He would force me to rethink my position and would argue that I should backtrack on what I'd promised her. And the basis for his argument would be solid, of course. Elle would always be the last White Rose, and we would always need to protect her from that.

I turned back to Sean. "Arrange for the helicopter to be flown here from Gatwick. Ben Scott will file the flight plan and clear French customs and pilot the aircraft. He'll retain possession afterwards and remain on standby until I release him."

"The countess will be well during the flight?" he asked.

"We'll conduct some test runs in this vicinity to be sure she can tolerate it. Since the cruising altitude is significantly lower and the cabin remains unpressurized, my money is on Elle. She'll do well." I grinned. "Let's get on with the meeting."

Elle's parents died in a plane crash when she was two years old, and that fact, compounded by the anxiety disorder she suffered from, made it difficult for her to fly in an airplane. The psychology of it manifested into a dangerous physical illness.

We hadn't discussed taking the helicopter yet, but I was confident that my wife would give it a shot. If she did refuse or if our test flights failed, then we'd take the car shuttle train through the channel tunnel. I preferred not to do that if she could acclimate to travel in my corporate helicopter.

"Good morning, Mr. Hastings. So nice to see you," one of the four lawyers said from a monitor on the wall. "Are you ready to open up your general partner stakes today?"

"I appreciate the light tone. As you well know, this was never in the business plan when Ethan and I created it. But Ethan is gone, and it's time for HG to become more progressive. Thomas and James have proven they can successfully carry operations when I am otherwise occupied.

"My brother is prepared to make a substantial investment as a senior managing partner, and James has accepted our offer for a position as junior partner. HG shall seek a second junior partner.

"Once all four partners are invested, the group will accept offers from funds management firms who wish to invest in the general partner stakes. The selected firm, if one is selected—and make certain that language is clear in the documents—would own a nonvoting stake and must provide a generous capital infusion, which would be used for new strategies such as expansion into credit and growth equity."

I signaled for Sean to get me another cup of coffee. "Thomas will now run through the division of new and existing office operations."

Thomas stood and walked to the opposite end of the room. He filled his cup, then leaned against the table and looked to the monitor. "We've offered management of the forthcoming Madrid office to James, and he has accepted. We expect to receive his start-up proposal within thirty days. I will open and run the New York office.

"My brother is set to launch Paris over the next twelve weeks. When our fourth partner comes on board, that person will assume responsibility for the Paris office. London remains HG's home office, and when Will is ready to step back from operations, I'll assume full management. When the time comes, the juniors will be given an opportunity to submit proposals for an additional office in Frankfurt.

"Keep in mind we have existing clients in each of these territories, so we're indicating the new offices are more than basic organizational start-ups. Each of the ops will hit the ground running with active accounts and investors."

"If I might add," James interjected. "There's quite a lot of untapped interest in the Madrid region—new markets, new capital opportunities—and I'm prepared to dive in when the senior partners believe we're ready to expand on that plan."

"Good. Let's get these contracts signed and get to it," I said.

Our lawyers walked us through the contracts, and each was fully executed. Hastings Group was a young company and becoming more progressive would take it to another level. I expected my own personal earnings to increase another 20 percent within the year.

My mind wandered while Thomas led the rest of the meeting.

Elle would be safer in France. Devon Parker's reach would be eliminated.

And I'd have more space to process the issue with Thomas—it was obvious he had feelings for my wife. Christ, but I needed him. Elle needed him. But the truth was, it would take only one lapse in my brother's judgment to tear this family apart. I was certain he understood that just as well.

Elle lifted onto her knee to lean over the console that separated our leather seats and braced herself with one hand on my thigh as she watched the deer run through the trees into the open grassland. She reached across with her other hand and touched her fingertips to the glass on my side of the helicopter. I had to kiss her—there was no fucking help for it when she was so near, so alive with curiosity and awe.

At least two dozen deer in the herd loped along, enjoying the warmth of the late afternoon sun, their heads disappearing now and then when they indiscriminately foraged through the tall grasses. Most of the winter coats had been shed. The brighter chestnut and the white spots made it easier to track them.

Elle pressed the corner of her mouth harder against my lips. "There she is," she announced through her headset. "I think it's her. . . . Wait—oh, yes . . . I see the crescent-shaped spot on her back. She's grown a lot. They've all grown so much, it seems."

"It was a good winter for the deer as well, then. The females should start giving birth over the next couple of months."

Ben had gradually climbed to four thousand feet and then made a gentle descent to less than a quarter of that altitude, and my wife was doing quite well with the new experience. Though it was just the three of us on board, the luxurious passenger cabin accommodated four, while the cockpit had room for two pilots.

"You're feeling okay, baby?"

"I'm great, actually," she said. "I'm ready to go closer to the channel."

I grinned. "Yeah?"

"It makes no sense. Flying should be flying, but this feels different to me."

"The loss of control doesn't weigh as heavily with the clear visibility that comes with these lower altitudes." I switched over to Ben's channel on my headset for a second. "We're doing well back here, my brother. Hit the beach. Keep it low."

"If hovering over the water scares you, Elle, we'll go back. Just say the word."

She sat back in her seat and gave me a double thumbs-up. And a smile. Christ, that goddamned smile. The one that was a contradiction of her innocence because it baited me with mischief at the same time and put my cock on notice.

I leaned over the console and stroked her bottom lip with my finger. "You know what I'll do to you . . . for smiling at me that way."

"Can he hear us, Will?" she asked, still with the smile.

I shook my head. "We're on our own channel. I have to switch over to talk to him."

"Hmm." She moved her eyes to my erection. "So, he wouldn't hear me if I commented on how hard you are right now . . . or if I told you how badly I want you to fill me and stretch me and make me come while you're inside of me?"

Yeah. I was going to fuck the hell out of my little tease when we returned home.

"You just made your bed, witch." I winked.

She giggled. "And I can't wait to lie in it beneath you, savage."

I ran my finger over her bottom lip again. I wanted to taste it, taste all of her, but instead, I angled my chin towards the glass beside her. The helicopter was hugging the coastline. We were about to move out over the water, and she hadn't noticed.

Her gaze bounced between the eroded sandstone walls on the

beach and the horizon, and she lost her breath for a moment. “It’s all just so beautiful from here,” she said. “Experiencing it this way makes it feel like it belongs to me.”

Only one beauty moved me.

“It does belong to you. Whatever you want, Elle. It’s all yours.”

Her fingertips found the inside of my forearm, and she traced the lines and the curves of my tattoo. The rose. The dagger. Her name. “You can’t give me the cliffs or the sea or the moon. Still, I know you would try. Why are you so good to me, Will? I’m not the perfect angel you believe you see. I’m flawed like everyone else. Perhaps even more so.”

Her green eyes. So unexpected. So fucking lovely.

“You are perfect to me. For me. And you *are* an angel. My angel. Attempting to convince me otherwise will never do. It will only serve to make me angry. And, Elle, you do know that about me.”

Whatever she was keeping from me was eating at her conscience. I had to make her see. There was nothing left that we hadn’t already endured that could break us.

She nodded and diverted her eyes to the west, searching the horizon for the Atlantic Ocean. “How are we this lucky? To be loved by the person we love more than ourselves. It’s difficult to understand, you know?”

“I don’t care to understand. How or why means nothing. I care only that it is.”

Ben tapped on the glass dividing panel between the cockpit and the cabin, and I switched my headset over to his frequency.

“Are we good back there? You ready to call it a day?” he asked.

“All is well. Take us home, Ben.”

I pulled Elle onto my lap. “You being able to do this . . . well, it opens up more possibilities for us. I don’t want to travel without you. I can’t live without you.” I kissed the tip of her nose.

She kissed my cheek. “Same.”

“You’re flying, baby.”

"It's really kind of crazy, right?"

We chuckled close to each other's mouth, and I took advantage of the near contact, pushing past her lips with my tongue to taste her, to kiss her until she couldn't draw another breath. . . .

Not until I gave it to her.

32

Vanity fucking *Fair*. I had forgotten about the interview and couldn't remember why we agreed to be featured in the magazine's celebrity spread in the first place.

Wanted to show the world my biggest win.

Elle and I were greeted by the publication's senior editor midway across the lawn after our exit from the helicopter. Sean led the woman to us, her stiletto heels sinking into the turf and her short, dark curls standing on end as she trudged in our direction.

"Hello! I'm so glad for the chance to see you today. Sean says you're leaving soon for Paris," she shouted above the noise as Ben piloted the small aircraft to one of the estate's outbuildings. "I'm Jenn Jackson. It's a pleasure to finally meet you both."

I shook her hand. "Will. This is my wife, Ellie. I understand you are James's sister."

"Yes, that's right. I just ran into my brother inside the house, which is quite amazing, by the way. You should know he loves working at your company." She spun on her heels to greet Elle, extending her hand again. "It's lovely to see you in person, Countess."

"Please. Call me Ellie. We're glad you could make it down from London. I thought it would be nice for you to visit Eastridge since so many of the photos were taken here."

I placed my hand on the small of Elle's back and nodded for Sean to lead Ms. Jackson back to the house. "We'll take a few minutes before we see you both in the drawing room."

"See you in about thirty minutes," Elle added. "Mrs. Bates will serve tea on the hour. Make yourself at home, and by all means, spend some time with your brother if you'd like."

Ms. Jackson stared for a second and seemed rather tongue-tied. It was the eyes. Newcomers were struck by the rare green shade of Elle's irises, and sometimes rendered speechless by her natural beauty. She was just as beautiful when the couture and the makeup and the cameras were gone.

I grinned and led my wife into the house.

What a lucky motherfucker I was.

"I'm not sure I'm looking forward to this interview." Elle caught her arm up in mine as we hit the staircase together. "Did you see the copy layout on your desk? The headline says 'Meet the New Plantagenets' or something like that. Who would even know what that means? I'm excited about the feature, but I don't want us to be called that."

"We'll tell her to change the headline."

"I don't think we can edit their publication."

"You know better, Elle. If you don't like it, it will be changed."

"I don't like it. This is the twenty-first century, and we're the *Hastings* family."

I stopped on the landing and pulled her hand to my mouth, smiling against her skin. "Before I asked you to marry me, I worried you might refuse to take my name. You were so head-strong when you were grieving. I thought you might feel like I was taking something more away from you, that you were losing your independence."

"That's thoughtful but wrong. My commitment to you and to

our family has nothing to do with gaining or losing independence. And for the record, you never asked me to marry you—you commanded it. Lucky for you, I was already determined to spend the rest of my life in your bed." She winked. "Oh. Now I can't stop thinking about how enormous your erection was on the helicopter. Sometimes I wonder how you manage to fit it inside your trousers."

I laughed. Really, truly laughed. Elle stared at me for a second, shocked, I think. Spontaneous laughter didn't exist for me before Elle. But there it was. She let out one of her own husky laughs, and I picked her up into my arms. Her long legs came round my waist, and she crushed her lips against mine.

"I love you, Will."

"That's all I want, Elle. That's everything I need."

I didn't kiss her back. Christ, I wanted to kiss her. But right then, the mobile in my pocket buzzed with a message we'd been expecting. Elle slid to her feet, and I read the text out loud.

Commissioner Brown: Parker's trial opens tomorrow morning.

Shit. Fact was, the commissioner had no way to guarantee a conviction. He had confidence in the case he had built against Devon Parker, but ultimately, he had no control over the court's ruling, even if he had provided solid evidence to the prosecutor.

A sharp pain cut through the center of me. The physical discomfort was a warning. Darkness stirred. My next thought? Shut down the *Vanity Fair* piece to limit my wife's public exposure until I killed that motherfucker.

THE LAST SECRET

From: Ellie <ellie.hastings@hastingsgroup.co.uk>
To: Isobel <isobel.james@hastingsgroup.co.uk>

This must be short because Will is waiting for me. We're leaving for France, but I need to tell you this first. I think the time is coming, Isobel. We must tell Lissie soon. I know I said it wasn't part of our plan, but a London tabloid has since speculated that you are a Hastings.

I'll let Will know when we reach Paris. Your brothers do not seem to have the desire to keep your father's secrets. I don't believe they will deny that you are one of them.

Lissie deserves the truth. And it should come from Will and me. She deserves to know where and to whom she belongs.

I will not watch her grow up lost and empty, longing for the love of parents she never knew—or living under a cloud of shame because people believe her mother and father were sister and brother.

I can give her more than that, more than we had, Isobel.

But I have to hurt her first to make her whole. Telling her that

Sarah Parker is her biological mother and that you are her aunt will not only confuse her, but also it will break her heart.

And you must know that I found yours and Ethan's final secret—something the commissioner unearthed for me. I will not say the words or write them down. Not yet.

But soon I will say the words to Will.

The last lies must be revealed.

For Lissie.

For you.

For her father.

33

Whirling blades lifted us from the ground as they beat the surrounding air into submission, and the engine forced us forward over the ridge. Within seconds, the helicopter was five hundred feet above our favorite spot on the beach, where Ben hovered to be sure my wife was ready for our thirty-five-minute flight across the English Channel.

Elle leaned back against her seat and smiled. The rhythmic *thwup* of the rotor system seemed to lull her. "I'm ready. I can't wait to see Boulogne-sur-Mer."

At night, when we were home at Eastridge, she often stared out beyond the east-facing windows in our suite, searching for the lights of the French coastal town opposite Hastings on the other side of the channel.

It came as no surprise to me how fascinated Elle was with the idea of Boulogne. The ancient seaport built by the Romans was France's largest fishing harbor. It was situated about twenty-five miles south of Calais, and as one would expect, the town's soul was connected to the sea. The vibrant, bustling markets, the seafood restaurants, and the striking Gothic cathedral—the minor basilica Notre Dame de Boulogne sur Mer—drew tourists all year long.

Ben had arranged for a private landing at the helipad owned by the hotel, where I planned for Elle and me to stay that evening after we explored the streets of Boulogne. It was an opportunity for us to take back our freedom in a place where no one would care who we were or how much money I had. We would be on our own for the first time. Elle deserved that and much more than I'd given her, and this was only the beginning. Paris was next.

Her eyes sparkled with wonder as she peered across the water.

She's so beautiful. Never get used to that.

Our aircraft climbed higher, easing into the crossing of the channel, and Elle was doing quite well. Ben rapped his knuckles against the glass partition without turning away from his control panel and held up two fingers, signaling for me to switch my headset over to his frequency.

"How's Ellie doing? Are we good to continue on to the Continent?" he asked.

"She's great. Take your time."

"I'm not pleased with this plan. At. All. Why don't I stay on in France for a week or two while Taylor gets his break? You need some level of security presence, goddammit. Even if it's just me."

"There was a day not so long ago when I was the only one with my head in this game. Look at you all now. My brother is angry, and you haven't stopped bitching for days. Listen. I've carefully considered the situation, and I would never risk her life if there was an immediate concern on the radar. There is nothing more important to me than my wife's safety, and you know it."

"You don't have to shut the rest of us out because you've hit one of your black fucking moods, my brother. I'm not blind. I see it stirring."

"We need some space, Ben. Elle and I need time alone. That's all it is. What I want from you is for you to remain 100 percent ready. If Devon Parker's sentencing and transfer occurs sooner than anticipated, or if he's acquitted, I'll need swift, undocumented travel to and from London, and it must be you who comes with me. I trust no one else."

"Thomas would stay in Paris with Ellie while we hit London," he said, nodding his approval. "Well, if you want me to leave you here alone, your arse better check in every goddamned day and keep me informed on the status of the trial."

"That I will do, my brother."

"Does she know?"

"Yes."

Elle understood what was going to happen. She knew quite well the man she'd married, and she knew what had to be done to keep her safe and our family whole. The details, the actual plan—that was something else. I would not share it with her, and she wouldn't ask me to.

"Alert me when we're five minutes from the helipad," I added.

I closed the privacy panel and switched back to the other headset channel, back to Elle.

Her fingertips stroked my forearm, and she flashed the smile that was always mine, her stare nailing me from beneath her long lashes. "Dance with me tonight."

Christ. The hairs on my arm raised on end.

"Of course, baby." I leaned over and pulled her face close to mine.

She continued to stare at me. "Don't kiss me. Not until we dance."

"What if I can't wait that long?"

"You must."

"Elle, don't tease me. You belong to me. I'll kiss that mouth and that pretty little cunt whenever I choose to, and you will beg me to do it again."

Fucking possessive egomaniac.

Short puffs of breath escaped from between her parted lips and blew against mine. It was warm and sweet and intoxicating. Her green eyes never left mine, even as she dragged her fingers along the waistband of my jeans until finding the button.

"I don't think you can call me a tease, Will, when you actually receive something."

Elle's eyes stayed with mine as she unfastened that goddamned button and lowered the zipper to free my erection. Her thumb swirled round the tip of my cock, and then she slid her hand down my shaft and up again, creating erogenous friction, making me harder.

A growl rumbled in my throat, and I thrust into her hand.

"You are a tease . . . because you know I can't have you in this helicopter."

Those eyes. Her gaze was still locked onto mine as she dropped to the floor on her knees and pushed between my legs. "Maybe you can. Maybe we can start our honeymoon right now."

I should have stopped her then. The strength to deny her was nonexistent. She owned me.

My wife took the head of my cock into her mouth, the tight warmth consuming me, and I let her. I groaned at the slide of her tongue. I cursed under my breath as she took more of me into her wet, velvety mouth and sucked hard. I sank deeper into the seat and dug my fingers into the back of her hair. That tongue and those plump lips were so fucking good, and I wanted more.

"Ah, Christ. . . ." Another erotic rush. She'd grazed the underside of my cock with her teeth. "God . . . damn . . . it . . . Elle." I didn't make her stop. I wanted more.

She sucked harder, pulling me in deeper until I hit the back of her throat. I couldn't keep from thrusting any longer. It was harsh, something I should never do to her, but I did it anyway. Tears collected in her eyes. It was too much for her.

Fuck. Make her stop.

I was mad with the desire to thrust more, harder, and was

close to coming. Christ, I wanted to come into her throat. But I would not do that to her. She'd have to ask me for it first. Plead with me. Demand it.

My breath was heavy, and my heart pounded violently.

I was close.

"Elle. Come to me." As painful as it was to pull out of her mouth, I yanked her from her knees onto my lap and drew her mouth to mine, worshipping that sweet little mouth with my tongue. I took the kiss I wanted. She had been warned.

She tugged at her clothing. "Rip this," she said, yanking at a strip of lace on her knickers.

I grabbed her wrists. "You know we can't do that here."

"Please, Will. We don't have much time. I want you now."

I smirked, pleased with myself for being the source of her desperation, and tore apart the lace. She would get what she wanted. Slowly, I held her hips and eased her down on me.

So fucking good. Heaven.

"I want all of you," she whispered, moaning as I stretched her.

I pushed deeper into her body and slid my hand between us to pleasure her more while controlling my thrusts. She writhed against my fingers. I growled.

"Slow and easy, baby. We don't want to break the aircraft and drop into the water."

She chuckled for a moment, then forced her mouth against mine and cried out, saying my name, pushing the vibration of the drawled syllable deep into my soul as her tight cunt clenched round me and we climaxed together.

34

It was our first full day in Paris. There were no personal protection officers, no weapons, no security details to sort through. The usual fear and anxiety Elle experienced eased the minute we had arrived in France. She never looked happier or more beautiful than she did lying beneath me, catching her breath. I held her hands against the mattress with our fingers entwined.

Two days earlier, she had sauntered gracefully along the cobblestoned streets of Boulogne with an ice cream cone in her hand. The brisk coastal air had cooled her cheeks and nose, and the pink belted coat she'd worn had complemented her rosy skin. Her eyes had been vibrant, the color brighter than usual, like rare aquamarine gemstones.

Elle wasn't the only one to revel in our hiatus from England. I had waited for the day when it would be me who walked beside her as she strolled through town eating ice cream. More than ten years before, in Connecticut, that was how I'd caught my first look into those eyes. I had set up the situation so she would bump into me on the crowded street. I had been desperate to see her face, to feel her skin, to know she was real. She'd thumped into my chest, and I'd touched her for the first time.

That was the day I swore she would become mine.

And now she was lying beneath me, all mine.

Our marital bliss, as Elle called it, wasn't something I could have imagined. Life before her had been a dark hell. The shit that had inhabited my father, and subsequently lived inside of me, controlled everything for years. His ghosts, now my ghosts, would always remain. But Elle was here now to light up my soul and show me the way whenever I was lost. Her unconditional love dulled the pain so that I could live with it and feel beyond it.

Only a fucking fool would take her for granted.

My wife continued to hold something back from me, though it no longer mattered. Whatever it was, it could be managed. Nothing would change how much I wanted to be with her or how deeply I loved her. My desire for Elle was like a primal instinct that affected every part of me.

Mine.

We were happy. The obscure cloud cover that lingered while Devon Parker was alive wouldn't last. I wasn't pleased by the idea of taking another life—one more sin to punish my conscience—but I couldn't allow Parker to continue breathing. Given an opportunity, he would come for Elle. He would never have the chance.

As for the other threat, Martin and I would continue our surveillance of the two monarchical extremists. No reports of activism had emerged from his reconnaissance or mine. Martin believed the potential for reformation hinged upon whether or not Elle had children with me.

Fuck that.

She wants my children, and she's going to have what she wants.

It was time for us to live for the present.

We were still in bed after arriving late in Paris the night before. We'd spent the morning making love and snacking on the food brought in by the maid service. The service had delivered enough hot breakfast and fruit and pastries to feed a dozen people.

The time alone was exactly what we both needed. Although we had agreed to delay our honeymoon, together we'd longed for it, ached for the rite that normal couples took for granted. And then a sudden sense of urgency had overwhelmed us.

Being normal was something we didn't know much about, but we were determined to experience it on some level while in France.

Elle freed her hands from mine and pushed on my chest with both palms, reminding me that she was bearing a great deal of my weight. "Get up, savage. You're crushing me. I have to pee. And I'm starving."

I dragged our sweating bodies together into an upright position and pressed her harder to my chest to feel the beating of her heart against mine. She hooked her legs tightly round my hips. My cock was still inside of her. The pulse in her neck caught my attention, and I was compelled to rest my lips there. I kissed her in that spot quite often.

Because her life was everything to me.

"You've eaten quite a lot already," I said against her skin. "Seems I found the trick to making you want a proper English breakfast. Need to fuck you every morning until you can't walk."

"Mmm, yes. But you would have to change the hours you keep at the office." I didn't need to see her face to know that my wife was smiling. It came from her heart. "I'm going to need that hot soak we talked about earlier. My thigh muscles are already screaming," she added.

"Be sure to hydrate as well. Our marathon's been a good work out." I sucked on her neck, on the little white birthmark she claimed was a butterfly. It was not. "Christ, what a bloody good morning."

"It's almost one o'clock. Morning has come and gone. What

shall we do with the rest of our day? You're not expected for business meetings for a few days . . . right?"

I pulled out of her. She groaned. I understood the sense of loss and placed a soft kiss on her lips. "We have the week before Sean arrives and meetings begin. You know, there is something we've never done together, and I'm a bit wound up over it."

Her swollen pink lips parted, opening for a quick, shallow inhale. "Oh. I haven't given you everything you need," she whispered.

Both corners of my mouth twitched. I allowed one to curve.

"You must tell me, Will. You can't just smirk and not say it. I'll do anything for you."

"I've warned you not to question how well you satisfy me in bed. I'm quite pleased. Can you not see that? If I want something different, you'll know when I take it from you."

"So what is it we haven't done that you want, then?"

I grinned. "Shopping."

She struck me playfully on the chest. "Damn it. You could have just said so."

I tossed her over my shoulder onto the mattress and kissed her neck over and over while tickling her sides until she giggled and writhed beneath me. "What fun would that be, my tough little wife."

"Stop . . . oh God, Will, I'm going to pee! Let me go!"

Collapsing onto my back, I allowed her to leave our bed. I watched the sway of her hips and her lovely arse as she made her way to the toilet. My handprints still marked her skin.

"I'll never fucking let you go," I said to the bathroom door.

My wife sat in the steaming bath between my legs with her back pressed against my chest, her head resting on my shoulder. She released a contented sigh. "I'm glad you joined me, Will. This is quite nice."

"It is." I rested my chin on top of her head.

She spun to face me, splashing water out of the free-standing copper tub. "We're actually doing it." She laughed. "This is a real honeymoon." Another husky laugh. "It feels weird. What do we do? Are we supposed to know how to do this?"

"We'll do whatever feels good. Nothing more, nothing less." A wisp of hair fell from her messy updo, and I twirled it round my forefinger.

"This apartment is amazing. Thank you for leasing something so wonderful."

With her eyes wide open, she pressed her lips to mine and held the soft kiss for a minute.

Sean had found us a quiet location known for its charming cafés, quaint bistros, and green spaces. When Elle and I had talked about where we wanted to stay, we'd decided on something out-of-the-way. Privacy. Space. No distractions. No goddamned gaping tourists. I would take Elle to any place in Paris, to any landmark or attraction she wanted to see. We didn't need those things outside of our windows.

The spacious apartment had a grand interior and classic glamour. The living spaces and bedrooms offered distinct period features and traditional French opulence, while the kitchen and bathrooms were modern. The flat was a lovely balance of old-world charm and contemporary comfort—complementary contrasts that reminded me of my wife's own beautiful blend of contrasting qualities.

"I want to tell you something, Will, but I don't want it to ruin our mood. We're happy. Tell me our holiday won't be ruined." Her tone was serious but not severe or frightened.

"You can tell me anything, baby."

"I received a call from Caroline. She wanted to let me know that one of the small tabloids printed something speculative about Isobel being related to you. Isobel's name was not used." She closed her eyes for a moment. "This time."

"We'll handle it."

"That's it?"

Elle dragged her finger over the top of my shoulder, tracing the scar there before moving to the two older blemishes on my chest. Her eyes hit the scar from the gunshot wound beneath my arm before her fingertips arrived to circle it. The way she worshipped my body and acknowledged the marks left behind by violence and death was a silent ritual of hers.

"Yes, that's it. I'll ring Thomas when we're out of the tub, and he will take care of it. See? Nothing has been ruined." I winked.

"Your body is like a work of art," she said with a sweet smile, tracing the outline of my pectoral muscles.

"You don't mind? I mean, some of the heavier muscle was lost during physical rehab."

"That's crazy, Will. I didn't fall in love with you because you're a big man. And really, I hate to break this to you, but you're still much larger than most men."

"Being six five does come with some advantages." I winked again. "Are you in the mood to buy some dresses today?"

I wanted to take Elle shopping at the finest French boutiques. She loved dresses and shoes and delicate lingerie, and her dressing rooms in both houses in England still had plenty of space to be filled.

A stylist generally created Elle's public image and designed her wardrobe.

But not in Paris, not with me. Elle would have free rein to rebel. She would choose whatever her heart desired.

BEAUTY AND HER BEAST

From: Ellie <ellie.hastings@hastingsgroup.co.uk>
To: Isobel <isobel.james@hastingsgroup.co.uk>

You came back to me last night, Isobel, but it no longer makes a difference that you come and go, because I've forgiven you for leaving me, forgiven you for lying. Ethan too. There's no longer another way for Will and me. We must forgive you. In time, your brother will forgive you and Ethan as I have.

Ethan once said something to me that resonates in my heart this morning. *Blood is blood . . . always to be protected . . . no matter the circumstances.*

Now I see how carefully Ethan articulated during our conversations, making sure his words to me weren't ever really lies at all. It makes me wonder if he hadn't intended all along for me to be the one who discovered what he'd done to protect Lissie.

We were different, he'd said when I had pushed him on whether or not he had loved you. Placing his words in context with his actions, I clearly see that he loved you in a different manner than Will loves me. Ethan loved you as a sister.

As misguided as Ethan's actions were all along, he believed he was protecting his family, that he was keeping Lissie safe while still watching over her. I suppose he had his own logic for what he did and for allowing us to assume you two were lovers.

It's no longer for my own losses that I grieve. It's for yours. A child, a husband, a life. You loved David, but never experienced an insane love like the one I have with Will.

I miss you, Isobel.

I wonder. . . . If I continue with our boy talks, can you hear me? Can you feel me?

Last night Will waited for more than an hour on the balcony of our apartment while I dressed for our first date in Paris. There are few things in life a man like Will can't control. How I present myself to him and the time it takes for me to feel comfortable with it belongs in that small category.

I came out of the master suite wearing dark makeup and a revealing black dress. He had moved the dining table and chairs from the center of the room to clear the space.

Will stepped inside onto the elegant parquet and asked for my hand. His eyes filled with stormy emotion as he explored the details of my body. His lips parted, but no words came from them. He wore black trousers and a crisp white shirt with the sleeves folded back to reveal his forearms, one covered with the tattoo that bears my name.

God, I couldn't wait to touch his clean-shaven face.

When I offered my hand, he did not pull me in for a kiss. He bowed, then raised our joined hands into the air above my head. I twirled beneath his arm, and he led me across the wood floor in a waltz. There was no music. Only what we heard in our own heads.

There is masculine grace and refinement about Will when he moves. It's marked with a predator-like edge. It is delightful and stirring.

My husband led me through a few dozen flawless box steps before lunging to the side to lower me into his arms. "You are so lovely," he said. He then bent his tall frame and pressed his lips to mine. "What you do to me . . . I can't find the words, Elle."

Your brother surprises me this way, with unexpected gestures that create romance in a timeless sense. No other man could love me the same. Only him.

I wish you could have known him.

35

After a second full day of shopping and wandering about Paris, Elle and I headed back to the apartment to change for dinner. We'd gone to a formal restaurant the evening before, but this time, we were planning a more casual meal. We hadn't hurried out of bed or rushed through any of our afternoon shopping sprees. The hired car was on my payroll for the duration of our stay, and the mature driver was native to the city, so he was wise to the best sights and shops as well as to the less congested routes.

Some of our packages would be delivered after custom alterations, and many others filled the sedan's boot. We would have to ship most of it home when we left France.

"You looked so handsome in the blue shirt and jacket combo, and it was perfect with the jeans you have on now. And for your eyes." She dragged her fingers along my five-o'clock shadow. I had surprised her with a clean shave the day before.

Without thought, I drew her hand to my mouth and kissed it, my words vibrating over her soft skin. "You all right, baby?"

"Fine. I'm happy, Will. Can't you tell?"

"I can. Me too." My lips moved to the inside of her wrist,

where the delicate blue veins were visible and her radial pulse confirmed she was real, that she was mine. "You're a little pale, is what I meant to say."

The chauffeur opened Elle's car door and dropped his chin. "Madame."

She looked back at me as she climbed out of the car. "You worry too much. I feel fantastic."

Better be the truth. Maybe she misses our girl.

I unfolded myself from the backseat and stepped onto the pavement beside her. "Let's call Lissie tonight. I'll send her some snaps of the ducks at the river just before we call."

Elle giggled. "If anyone ever looked at the photos on your phone, they would never believe you were the dangerous man that you are."

"Dangerous? You must have me confused with someone else, angel." I winked at my wife and grabbed her hand as we hit the stairs for the apartment. "Christ, I'm hungry. You hungry?"

"Starving. Find us a place while I get changed? The weather is amazing again today. Another walk through the city this evening?" She grinned.

Before I let her slip away to the bedroom, I pulled her body against mine. "Kiss me before you leave me, Elle." But I didn't give her the chance. The back of her head was already in my palm, and I forced her mouth to mine, pushing beyond those luscious pink lips.

It was a fierce, no-holds-barred kind of kiss. I dove deep into her sweet taste, fucking her mouth with my greedy tongue, urging her to meet me with the same passion.

Elle broke the kiss and panted against my cheek for a moment. She pulled back and hit me with her eyes. "I will never leave you, Will."

She knew me so well. She knew exactly what I'd wanted.

Reassurance. Demanding it was unfair to her, but my heart

required it. I lived with an overwhelming fear that someday, in some way, I would lose her.

I had done the same thing to her the night before.

The moon had been high and the breeze warm when we'd left the restaurant. We had decided to walk round the city for a while before driving back to the apartment. We had ended up along the scenic walkway of the Right Bank. The city had been fully awake, the reflection of its lights dancing on the Seine. What was more, the way the moonlight had painted the contours of her face, her body, the way it had clung to her long hair as we walked along the river had taken my breath away.

After leaving the riverbank, I'd backed her into a dim alcove and pressed her body against a brick building with mine.

Lock your arms round my neck, and do not remove them, I had said.

Her breath had quickened as she submitted to me. As she had breathed out, I had breathed in, her rhythm completing mine.

I need to touch you . . . now . . . here. You will be quiet. Because you are mine. Your moans, your cries—all mine.

Her pupils had grown large, and her breath had accelerated.

I need to touch you too, she'd whispered close to my ear.

Not this time. I had tucked my thumb under her chin, pulled her mouth to mine, and sucked on her bottom lip. *Your hands are exactly where I want them to stay. Understand?*

She'd nodded, and I had dropped my hand, sliding it up her thigh beneath the hem of her dress. When my fingers had brushed the lace on her knickers, a small whimper had hit her throat.

Covering her mouth with mine, I had kissed her savagely. She'd met my tongue with hers, falling into the moment with me. I had pushed my fingers inside of her, wringing a soft cry from her against my lips.

Come for me, baby. Melt into my hand.

I had wanted to watch. See her lids drop, her head fall back, her skin bloom with heat, and her lips part until her mouth formed a circle that was too small for my rigid cock. I'd wanted to hear the puffs of exhalation that she couldn't control, to feel her erotic little scream as I captured it with my own mouth.

She had done all of those things, and I had nearly come in my trousers.

Sweat had soaked my clothing. My erection had been painfully hard, and I'd ached for release. The urge to feel her soul complete mine had been more than I could stand. That'd been my punishment for all the horrible shit I'd done, for the selfish acts I had committed—to watch something so beautiful, to hold someone I loved more than myself without taking anything from her, to drown in my own desire.

You're my world, Elle. Without you, it would end.

I won't let it end. I'm yours, Will. Always.

About an hour later, after Elle had freshened up and slipped into a casual dress for dinner, she and I walked hand in hand through the middle of the brick-paved streets until we heard the lapping waves of the River Seine.

The comforting aromas of freshly roasted coffee and sugared brioche and vanilla cream drifted out to the street as we passed by one of the city's thousands of cafés.

Neighborhood flower markets lined the pavements along the way. I'd noted one in particular earlier that day, located close to Pont Neuf, the bridge we would cross on our way to dinner.

I pulled Elle along by the hand as I weaved through that market's tables and floral displays, plucking individual fresh-cut flowers from tubs filled with water. When she realized that I was creating a hand-picked bouquet for her, she blushed. I grinned.

"Je veux une rose blanche parfait," I said to the market owner.

"Les roses sont à l'intérieur." The woman scuttled inside and

came back holding an exquisite white rose over her arm. "I grow the roses myself," she added.

"It's beautiful," Elle said.

The woman met my wife's eyes with a smile. *"Merci, madame."*

Elle hooked her arm in mine after I paid for the flowers, and we headed for the bridge. Pont Neuf was the oldest bridge in Paris. It was made of stone, with architectural arches and ornamental mascarons along the length of the exterior wall. Displaying sculpted mythical faces in that way seemed strange to me, but it had always been part of the sixteenth-century design.

The old stone bridge offered a paved walkway for pedestrians in both directions. The two stretches of walkway offered stone niches with wide benches where people could duck out of the foot traffic to admire magnificent views of the Louvre and the Notre Dame Cathedral or steal a kiss.

"You are the only man who's ever given me flowers, Will." The words were soft and honest, followed by a childlike smile. "There is only you," she added in a whisper.

There it was—the innocence that drew me into her deeper with each passing day. It was light and goodness and lived infinitely within her soul. It was what held me together through the madness. Her innocence healed me . . . completed me. I was addicted to it, and the craving was nonstop. I longed day and night to possess it, to possess *her*.

Unfortunately, there was no help for it or for me. The compulsion had to be satisfied. In an abrupt move, I pulled Elle into my arms and backed us into a niche to kiss her.

I owned her mouth with the same fierce passion as I had earlier, before we'd left the apartment. Something more was building between us, if that was possible, and I had no idea how or what the fuck it was. I only knew that there was more for us.

"Will," she whispered, her eyes full of unshed tears. She panted from the kiss. The sweetness of her breath hit me and caused the hair on my arms to stand on end.

Her tears started to fall.

The tears were different. No fear or pain or grief tainted them.

Something else overwhelmed her.

"Will," she said again.

I held her face in my hands, wiping her cheeks with my thumbs. Tears fell faster. They wouldn't fucking stop. I kissed her lips. "You don't have to say anything, Elle. Please don't cry."

She smiled through the watery sentiment. Her green eyes were brilliant, but those goddamned tears were still spilling down her face. "I think I should see a doctor right away."

My heart stopped. My body became one with the bridge. Immovable stone. "What?"

I stared at her and raked a hand through my hair. What the fuck was she saying?

She said my name again.

It was all I needed then, to understand—my name on her lips, lingering in the air between us with the softness of a tender love song.

"I think you should sit down," she said.

I shook my head. "I need for you to sit."

Elle lowered herself onto the stone bench, and I crouched between her knees. Our eyes locked. Her tears had not stopped.

"The test results weren't accurate."

I dropped my head onto her lap. "Oh, Christ," I said against the smooth fabric of her dress.

My wife's fingers pushed into my hair.

"We're pregnant."

I shook my head again, my face buried in the folds of her dress. "It's too soon, Elle."

Her fingertips moved gently through my hair. "Do you remember when you gave me this engagement ring, and I said the same thing to you—that it was too soon? You assured me it was not, and you were right. It took me a minute, but I realized that fighting what's meant to be is painful. And you and I already live with enough pain that is beyond our control."

Clever little angel. She was chucking my rationale back at me.

I lifted my head and met her eyes. She was calm and fearless. Her beautiful face was fuller and her skin was radiant.

So beautiful.

I had misinterpreted the signs as a manifestation of her anxiety.

"You're going to be a father, Will."

I drew breath through my nostrils and nodded on the exhale.

"We'll find a way to be happy about it together," she added.

36

Several days later, Elle hopped down from the examination table and into my arms. The doctor had performed an ultrasound and confirmed she was eight weeks into the pregnancy. She rested her cheek against the center of my chest and chuckled. "God, I should have known. Everything you do is bigger and better and more."

I secured my arms tightly round her warm body, and we swayed together as if there were music and we were dancing. A chuckle of my own vibrated in my throat. I inhaled against her hair. "Ah, well, you know me. You ask for something, and I give it to you in spades."

Christ. We were having twins.

We'll find a way to be happy about it together, she had said, her words loving and gentle.

Elle was right. Together we would find our way through this pregnancy and beyond with our children. It would take more work on my part than hers to find comfort and balance as a parent, but I could feel us shifting in that direction rather quickly.

None of it was going to be easy. Not for Elle and not for me.

There was still a lot of shit for me to sort through in my head, and my wife would not be fooled. She would see my struggle and feel my pain, so there was no reason for me to lie about it.

She lifted her head and nailed me with those eyes.

I placed a soft kiss on her lips. And another. One more.

"We'll work through this together," she said. "I'm scared too. But I know we can do this. You're already a better father than you know, Will. Look at how well you love Lissie."

"She's easy to love. What if the twins are like me?"

Elle grinned. "I'm counting on it. You can stop giving me things now."

"I'll never stop. And be careful what you wish for, angel. More of my likeness may not serve you well. Now, how about some lunch? We can go find something on the river."

"Could we go back to the apartment and order something in? I'd prefer to resume our Netflix-slash-honeymoon-sex binge."

I smirked. "Would you? As it happens, that's my preference as well."

Thomas was waiting at the apartment when we arrived. The fact that he'd left England and arrived on the Continent without a word in advance was not a good sign. He stood at the far end of the flat in front of the open balcony with his back to us, his hands braced on either side of the doorframe.

Elle and I stopped dead in our tracks and gaped from the foyer. My arm was extended in front of her body to shield her, a reflex of my protective instinct.

Christ. He was huge. He'd been training hard in the months since I'd been shot. My brother was an inch and a half shorter at six foot four, but he was now broader than I had been.

"Brother," I called out across the open rooms.

I couldn't see his face when he turned. He was silhouetted by the daylight behind him.

"Thomas, what are you doing here?" Elle asked. "You didn't call."

He started towards us, his features coming into view as the interior lights hit him. A smile hit his mouth and his eyes. He always lit up for her.

Elle ran to him then, and Thomas opened his arms to catch her. He glared at me over the top of her head as he held her, and the full force of his truth punched me in the fucking gut. He'd never been furious with me over the security issue because he understood that her safety was my lifeline. He was angry because I'd taken her so far away from him.

Elle pulled back from Thomas's embrace and punched him in the arm. "Damn you, Thomas. Next time, return my call."

My wife and my brother had been close from the beginning. She loved him. He was the protective big brother she'd never had. The shoulder she'd cried on when I'd let her down.

Thomas stared at me as he rubbed his biceps, feigning a sting from Elle's punch to humor her. "I wanted to surprise you."

"You two piss me off with your scheming." She turned to me. "Did you know he was coming, Will?"

I grabbed her hand and returned Thomas's hard stare. "I did not. My brother failed to check with me before crashing our holiday."

"Oh." Elle's eyes moved between Thomas and me. She squeezed my hand to let me know she recognized the tension. "I'm going to lie down for a few minutes while the two of you talk."

Neither of us spoke. I hit the bar and filled two lowball glasses with Scotch as we waited for the bedroom door to close.

Thomas tossed a copy of *Vanity Fair*'s latest edition onto the bar. Elle and I were on the cover. "You were supposed to cut the feature until Devon Parker was dead. We agreed on that. We agreed to block her exposure until then."

I opened to the magazine's center spread and unfolded a stunning photo of Elle in her wedding gown. She was standing outside the estate chapel at Eastridge. She was amazing. I couldn't drag my eyes away from the centerfold. "We agreed, Thomas. But my wife did not."

"What? Goddammit . . . what the—she doesn't get to make those decisions." He slammed his empty glass onto the bar. "Seriously, what the fuck is wrong with you?"

I stepped into my brother's space to intimidate him. More muscle strength or not, he didn't live in the same dark place that I did. An inhuman sound rumbled inside my chest. "Fuck off, Thomas."

He didn't blink nor had I expected him to. He was a Hastings. "You need to tell me when your resolve begins to weaken so you can leave the affected matter with me," he said through narrowed eyes.

I reached for my glass and shot the whisky. "My resolve is strong. You must remember that even if Elle is physically weaker than we are, her will is as strong as ours. And what's more, as you've said yourself, she is my partner, not my prisoner."

"I know how you love her, that you can't deny—"

"You *know*?" I snarled, cutting him off. I couldn't stop my fucking self. Every turn, another threat. Another way to lose her. And my brother was now part of that hell. "Tell me, Thomas. How would you know how I love her . . . what it *feels* like to love her?"

His eyes abruptly hit the floor, and he said nothing.

"I'll answer for you. You believe you know what it feels like because you're in love my wife."

Thomas shook his head, lifting his eyes from the wood planks but not high enough to reach mine. "She belongs to you. She's my sister."

"But you fucking love her. This goddamned pact our father put on us, being her defender, it fucks with your brain. It becomes a madness, makes you feel things. I left her with you twice. And now . . . you love her."

Fucked up as it was, I needed him to love Elle, because if anything ever happened to me, he would keep her safe for that reason alone. But not this way. He couldn't love her this way—not while I still had breath in my body. The possessive monster dwelling within me wouldn't allow it.

"I'm sorry, Will. It's not what I wanted, to love her this way. I fucking hate that I do."

The pain in his heart was clear. He'd already accepted his crime. It hit me then. Who was I to blame him for doing the same thing I'd done, for falling in love with a woman neither of us deserved? But still. . . .

"To be clear, know that I would kill you just as I would any other man."

Thomas met my eyes. "I will never touch her like that."

"Then find a way to change the nature of what you feel for her. Figure it out. And understand that it's not going to be easy. Not at all."

He nodded, and I pulled him into my arms.

"I trust you, Thom. Don't prove me wrong." And I did. I loved Thomas. But I loved her more.

"I won't let you down," he said as he pulled away.

We paused for a moment. Thomas spoke first.

"I think you might want to read that article. You're not going to like it."

"What's the problem?"

"It exposes Isobel as our sister."

"What?"

"Yeah. I bought the story from the tabloid, but *Vanity Fair* must have had the same source. Isobel's name wasn't used here either, but it's only a matter of time. I don't think there will be any real consequences when she is identified, since we're not in the business of covering for the old man anymore. But . . ."

"But Lissie."

"We know Isobel wasn't her mother, but the rest of the world doesn't know that," Thomas said.

Elle appeared in the doorway. "We have to tell Lissie before she hears it somewhere else. Then we'll inform the rest of the world on our own terms."

Thomas and I exchanged a deliberate look.

Shit. How much did she hear?

"I've been thinking about it since Caroline's phone call, Will. I don't want Lissie to grow up believing she was a child of incest. She deserves to know the names of her biological parents and where she belongs."

Elle came to the bar and pushed a bottle of sparkling water in front of me so I could open it for her. Then she poured more Scotch for Thomas and me.

Her behavior made it clear that she hadn't heard the first part of the conversation. It needed to stay that way.

I sat on a barstool and pulled her onto my lap. "I think you're right. We'll put the information out there and be done with it."

She nodded. "What else did I miss?"

"I haven't shared our news, if that's what you mean. I waited for you."

Our news about the pregnancy would push Thomas to fight harder to get beyond his feelings for her.

"Go ahead, baby," I whispered at her ear. "We've got this."

She twisted to see my face. We shared a knowing smile.

"Well, Thomas, you're going to be an uncle. Again, I mean. We're pregnant," Elle said. The happiness in her voice was profound. And goddammit, infectious.

"Wait—what? You're having a baby?" Thomas closed his eyes for a minute and then smiled. He and I were on the same page.

This would help him move forward with his own life. "Congratulations," he added. "You're both happy?"

Elle looked up at me again.

"Yeah. We are happy," I said, kissing the tip of her nose. "Twins. We found out today."

"No shit? Christ, woman, you'll grow bigger than a house," he teased.

"Don't make me kick your ass, buddy. You've already interrupted my honeymoon, so—"

"There'll be no arse kicking. No more fighting for you, Ellie."

"You finally get your wish, Thomas. No more fighting for me."

"Look. There's another reason I'm here," he said, redirecting his focus, his expression sobering. "Director Martin sent me."

37

Thomas let himself into the apartment the next morning and joined me on the balcony, where I watched Elle as she painted below in the private garden. He leaned on the wrought-iron railing next to me and slapped me affectionately on the back. "She's glowing," he said.

He was quiet for a minute as we stared down at the woman we loved. I was about to leave her with him again, and even though it was for only one evening, it was a difficult pill to swallow. Yet necessary.

"I'm proud of you, brother. You are a good husband, and you'll be a damn good father."

I turned the empty coffee cup in my hand. "We'll see, Thom." That his declaration was about him and me rather than about her helped ease the anger I suppressed. He was demonstrating that he could be trusted.

"You'll always have John and me. We've got your back. Listen. I've decided to spend some time in New York after this. I'll be as close as a phone call. If you need me for anything, just say the word, and I'll get on a plane and come home straightaway."

We still watched her.

Elle's hand guided the brush she held over the canvas in the same gentle rhythm she used when she created imaginary works on my chest. Goose bumps raised on my skin at the thought of her touch. I couldn't hear it, but I could see by the way her full lips were set together that she was humming a tune. She never failed to take my breath away.

The garden below our apartment had low boxwood borders and a smooth granite square in the center. There were a couple of benches for occupants seeking peaceful reflection. Mature tree branches reached over the square and met in the middle, their fluffy cherry blossoms merging into one large canopy. An iron staircase led from our balcony to the garden.

Elle smiled to herself, causing my own lips to curve.

"Let me do this for you, Will. I can head back to London immediately and take care of Devon Parker according to plan. Your place is here by her side. Stay in Paris with your wife and your babies."

I turned to him. "I need this one . . . need the closure. You'll keep my family safe until I return in the morning. Then you will go spend that time in New York . . . and you will do whatever it takes to find your way to the other side of your feelings for my wife."

He nodded.

"John will stay with me over the summer holiday," I added.

"He will be glad for the time with you. You've been John's father all along, you know. He respects you, loves you more than he did our father or Ethan."

"They never gave him enough attention."

My gaze went back to Elle.

She looked up to the balcony and smiled at me. Right then, I hoped like hell she would never come to know that my brother loved her as anything other than a sister. She waved at him before calling out to me. "I'm done for now. Can you come get the easel?"

"Be right there, baby."

Thomas cut in. "I'm going back to the hotel so you two can spend time alone before you leave. Ben will arrive on the Continent between six and seven o'clock. I'll be back here at seven. And brother, prepare her this time, goddammit."

"She understands."

Thomas walked away, leaving me alone with the image in my head of how I had hurt her more than once in the past . . . because I hadn't given her enough credit for the strength she possessed. I'd kept her in the dark, believing at the time that I was protecting her. She was almost killed. The scars on my body from a bullet reminded me every day that I had fucked things up.

That would never happen again.

After carrying Elle's easel and supplies into the apartment, I led her by the hand into the bedroom. Our bedrooms were the safe havens for our relationship, the foundation of our connection, the places where the world round us burned down but we survived as one whole. I needed her to feel us that way when I made clear what was going to happen that night.

Elle stood before me, her eyes locked into mine. I gave a gentle tug on the soft blue scarf she wore and brought it to my face to inhale her scent. Then I wrapped it round my fist.

Green eyes. Unshed tears. A sharp rush of air hit her throat, and she choked on it.

She understood my message. When I arrived in England later, the darkness I had caged for months—the rage she feared—would consume me, and I would become a killer again. I would take Devon Parker's life with my fists.

"I'm leaving with Ben for London at seven this evening. You will remain here inside this flat with Thomas. You have my word that I'll return to you at first light. You will not leave my brother or this apartment for any reason. I need to know that you are here waiting for me. Do you understand me, Elle?"

"I do," she whispered.

"And do you understand how I love you . . . and how being away from you feels like having a blade rip through my chest?"

"Yes. It's the same for me."

I bowed my head and stuffed her scarf into my pocket.

She placed my palm on her face. Her luminous skin was warm and soft as she brushed it against my hand. Her eyes burned, never leaving mine.

Message received. She was demanding that I come back to her, and what was more, she was showing me that I must return as the man who stood before her in that moment, not as the broken, ill-tempered man I'd once been. The rage had to die with Devon Parker.

"You are mine, Elle. I will always return to you."

She smiled. "You better, because I love you madly." My wife's lips came to mine, and I opened my mouth, allowing her to lead us into a passionate kiss.

Resting my forehead against hers after breaking our kiss, I told her that I loved her, told her no words were good enough to describe that love.

"Will, before you go, we should talk about another lie Ethan and Isobel kept from us."

"Because you believe I'll have more anger to purge from my system later?" I was teasing, but when her serious face confirmed that that was actually what she was thinking, my stomach shot up to my throat.

Her secret.

The lie she was keeping had never been about the pregnancy. There was something else.

"Yes," she said.

Elle entwined her fingers with mine and guided me across the room. Her eyes remained on my face as we lowered ourselves onto the settee at the foot of the bed.

I wiped the sweat from my brow and stared at my wife's mouth as she stumbled through the sentences. We could do this together, she was telling me. It wasn't as bad as it might sound. Something beautiful was the outcome. I should focus on the present and forgive the past transgressions of Ethan and Isobel. My brother. My sister.

Elle retrieved her purse and came back to the small sofa. She pulled out a photo she had never shared with me and placed it on my leg. "Do you recognize this woman?"

I lifted the photo. I did recognize her.

"Rebecca something or other. Hill . . . Rebecca Hill. She worked for David Nielson's father. You know David and his wife, Caroline, of course. Where did you get this?"

Elle didn't say a word. She wanted more from me.

"You want me to tell you about a woman who I saw only once years ago. She meant nothing to me. I don't follow this, Elle. It's not like you. Let's get back to the matter at hand."

"Tell me what you know about Rebecca Hill first."

It wasn't clear why she wanted to dive into my past with other women, but the determination in her expression was sharp and relentless.

"There's not much to tell. I met her at one of Mr. Nielson's dinner parties. Ethan and I were working on our business plan for the firm, and Nielson had connections. I'd attended Oxford with David, and apart from Ben, he was my closest friend at the time."

"More," she half-whispered.

"David and I stepped outside to get high. Rebecca followed. She and I hooked up after Nielson's dinner party, then she chased me round for months. I wasn't interested. I had no feelings for her, and I didn't care for her lifestyle. That is all."

"What do you mean when you say 'her lifestyle?'"

I tossed the photo onto a cushion. I'd never told Elle about the drugs. "What is it you discovered about Ethan?"

She narrowed her eyes and waited.

Fuck.

I dropped my face into my hands and pinched the bridge of my nose. "She was using cocaine quite a lot. Getting high served a specific purpose for me, and I didn't want to share that with a woman. It was how I managed my longing for you and pushed through the chaos when there was little time for sleep as we built the company."

"I see." She paused. It felt like days before she spoke again. "Did you sleep with her that night?"

"Yes."

Elle was quiet again. I found her hand and squeezed it.

"Will. The woman in the photo . . . it's Sarah Parker."

I jumped to my feet and met her eyes. "What? No. It's not."

Standing as well, she placed her hands on my forearms. She meant to soothe me.

"Please listen to me," she whispered. I nodded. She continued, "I will explain, I promise. But I'm begging you to consider everything we have now, all that is at stake for us, before you react. I need your word that you will listen and process and work through this with me."

"You're scaring the bloody fuck out of me, Elle, but I trust you. You have my word."

There was a faint spark in her eyes right then.

"Lissie . . . is your daughter. Yours, not Ethan's."

38

Several hours later, Ben piloted the helicopter across the channel, and I used the ride as an escape to pull myself together before we arrived in London. My best friend understood something more weighed on my thoughts, and he gave me the space to process it.

Elle had taken the photo of Sarah from Mrs. Parker's flat when I'd been outside making phone calls. She hadn't known at the time that Sarah was linked to me. But in the following days, as we had prepared for our travel, Commissioner Brown had provided her with more information.

The commissioner had not only continued interrogating Devon Parker for Elle, but he'd also investigated the lab where the DNA testing had been processed. My clever fucking brother had used my hair sample for the paternity test and had run it through one of the forensics labs. An involved employee who'd been fired thought he might earn a living from exposing this type of restricted information—otherwise the truth might have never been uncovered. The man had since been put behind bars.

I had dropped to the floor in a state of shock after Elle said the words—when she'd told me that Rebecca Hill was Sarah

Parker and Lissie was my daughter. There was no doubt in my mind that Elle's words were true. She would never say it without knowing it was the truth.

We stayed that way for quite a long time: me on my knees with my goddamned face buried in her warm body like I'd done when she'd told me we were pregnant, and Elle speaking tender words, holding me as she worked to ease my pain and confusion.

Time. I was banking on more of it before the twins were born. More time for me to find the place inside of me that would teach me how to be a good father. That thought process was wrong. Elle often warned me not to count on time, to cherish the days we had. *She* was that place inside of me. It was Elle who would show me how to be the kind of father I wanted to be for our children. Her belief in me was my guide.

Elisabeth Anne Hastings was my biological child.

While Elle and I had lain on the bed holding each other, she had relayed to me everything the commissioner had learned from his research and additional interrogations of Devon Parker.

My lovely, merciful wife believed my brother thought he was doing the right thing, that he was providing the best protection for Lissie by taking her from a drug-addicted birth mother and placing her with another Hastings—Isobel, who had just then miscarried her own child.

Elle had explained that, according to the commissioner, Ethan's decision to keep Lissie from me was said to have been motivated by my obsession with Elle. Allegedly, Ethan had insisted that I would never accept Lissie because she was connected to George Parker—the man who had attempted to kill Elle when she was eighteen. George had failed, of course, because my father had intercepted the Order's plan and killed him.

Ethan had paid Simon Parker to take the baby from his sister and had made regular payments to Simon for years. It wasn't until Ethan discontinued those payments that Simon had joined the Order to seek vengeance for the break in their financial arrangement.

Devon had suggested to the commissioner that I'd destroyed his sister with my rejection.

"Rebecca Hill" never informed me that she was pregnant.

Blood is blood, no matter the circumstances, and I would never reject my own.

Ethan should have known that. Elle insisted that I forgive him. I made her no promises on that front, but I would make the effort to move towards forgiveness for her sake and for Lissie's.

One question lingered. Simon and Devon had never expressed a desire to avenge their father's death. Perhaps it was because my father had lost his own life on a mission just four months after he had killed George. In the end, it had been money that had driven Simon, and Simon's death that had motivated Devon.

I was now on my way to take from the authorities the one man alive who could confirm it all, and after he gave me that corroboration, I would take the motherfucker's life as well.

Martin was waiting inside the old warehouse when Ben and I arrived on foot. We'd left the car several blocks away. I removed my sweatshirt hood and pounded on the metal door with the side of my fist four times before Martin opened it and gestured with his head for us to step inside.

He and another intelligence agent from his team were set up near the back wall under a single light bulb that hung above a stack of old wooden crates. The two men leaned over a large map that was spread out across the width of the improvised table.

"As you know, custody of Devon Parker was assigned to two officers of a private extradition company contracted by the Ministry of Justice," Martin said. "We've surveilled these men, and they would be no match for you and Ben should they offer resistance."

There would be no resistance because both men were on my payroll for the night. Martin was either unaware or wanted the rest of us to believe that he was. It was expected behavior for the sake of protecting the agent he'd brought into the fold with him.

"Parker will be alone in the back of the van, is that still correct?" I asked.

"Yes. He has been isolated due to the serious nature of his conviction and mental evaluation, and his transfer is scheduled for 2:00 a.m. to minimize any potential risk to civilians and peripheral employees." Martin frowned. "The commissioner tells me the man has quite a vile mind. Observe caution when you take him from the vehicle and otherwise."

I leaned over the map to examine the extradition company's planned route from London to the receiving facility in Northern England. "You might find some comfort when you recall my experience and who it was that trained me, Director."

"Quite."

Martin was well aware of my history.

"What about police escorts? Cars, sirens, anything that might draw attention to the transport van?"

"You should be clear of those obstacles. Generally speaking, a transfer like this one involves two cars or more, but not in this case. The minister of state himself ordered these terms, as recommended by the commissioner."

It wasn't lost on me that Commissioner Brown had a hand in this too. He and his sister, Caroline, cared about Elle. Nor was it lost on me that the minister, who was responsible for oversight of prison operations, sentencing, and public protections, was a known supporter of the prime minister and therefore of the Crown's back door into state business. It all meant one thing—the Crown still had my back.

"Send your cleanup team for the body one hour before dawn," I said.

Martin extended his hand. "It will be taken care of. . . . Good luck."

The feel of flesh against my fists consumed me. The grinding and snapping of splintering bone. Pooling blood. I was rage and it was me. Madness. There was nothing else.

Devon Parker had spoken my wife's name, and with that one word, all that I was collapsed beneath the weight of the darkness that lived inside of me. My mind broke, and the cage door flew open, freeing the feral beast—the part of me that existed only to protect her.

I had warned him, told him not to say her name.

During our "conversation," Parker claimed that he had targeted Elle to avenge his brother, Simon. He admitted he'd sent someone to the gala to scare her.

I walked round his body. He hung from a rafter by his wrists. Another sharp blow to his kidney.

A tortured howl, laboring breath, sweat.

Parker showed no sorrow for the loss of Sarah's life or remorse for having conspired with his brother to sell her child to Ethan.

"She was your fucking sister," I said, striking his face again.

"Our sister was Simon's weakness, not mine." Blood ran from his nose and the corners of his mouth. "I never cared for that bitch. She left us more than once. Fucking whore left us!"

His anger and his physical pain continued to rise, and in turn, he corroborated everything Elle had said.

He went on about how much he'd loved his father. George Parker had made his sons promise not to join the group of assassins he had served. He'd wanted them to care for their mother and sister instead. Never happened. Sarah was dead and their mother abandoned.

"You didn't even do that, you goddamned worthless fuck. But here's something you can take to your grave tonight. Your mother is in my care now." Parker flinched, and I flaunted a menacing grin. "I moved her out of that shithole you left her to die in and gave her money."

That's when he said Elle's name.

I cut the rope, and he dropped to the decaying cement floor.

Parker blathered unintelligibly, slurring, crying out for mercy as I pounded into his flesh and bone and spilled his blood, but his words had no effect on me.

Because I was rage, and there was nothing else.

I beat him to death with my bare fists.

Still on my knees, crouched over the lifeless body, I straightened my back and lifted my face to the sliver of moonlight peering through the damaged roof.

I had never heard the whispers, never felt the stars or the moon reach out to me. Elle's murmurs, her breath, and her radiance were the only peace that I'd known. Without her touch, the only release from my grim hell was stillness. I closed my eyes to wait for the silence.

Emptiness swept through my mind, then Elle's piercing green eyes were there. Thoughts of how I loved her and how she loved me filled my cold heart. It warmed my body and gentled the ghosts of my sins. The silence came as rage crept back into its prison at the bottom of the darkest part of my soul.

I opened my eyes and stood. My mind was clear, though a tormenting symphony of anger, guilt, shame, and sorrow still played in my heart. I pulled Elle's soft blue scarf from my pocket and held it against my face so I could inhale her scent. I wrapped it round my broken, bloodstained hand.

Getting back to her in Paris was all that mattered now.

Elle would make the pain in my soul stop.

My angel filled me with her light and her unconditional love. She fixed my broken pieces, showed me how to hold onto the beautiful moments we created, how to forgive, how to be a better man.

Elle made me see that I was more than a soldier of fortune, that I was no longer my father's trained killer.

She made me want to be a good father to my three children.

She made . . . me.

EPILOGUE

ELLIE, THREE WEEKS LATER

Will's car ascended to the top of the ridge, the soundless roar of the engine comforting me. The stone chimneys of the elegant family fortress I'd been longing to see came into view, and it was like reliving a beautiful dream. We were home. Along the side of the estate's private access road, vibrant blue flowers spilled out from between the trees, overwhelming areas meant for grass, as if there was no more earth left to carpet within the woodland.

Bluebells.

Hundreds of little flowers with their upturned tips hung from curved stalks that seemed to nod in our direction, bowing to their master to welcome him as he passed by them.

I couldn't wait to step out of the car and take in the sweet scent of the wildflowers, to inhale the brisk air blowing in from the northeast that would be fortified with the salt of the North Sea.

Paris had been an amazing experience and a wonderful, life-changing period of time for Will and me. We'd even contemplated for a New York minute what it would be like to stay there, where no one cared about my bloodline or even worried about the survival of the British monarchy. But it wasn't home, and in fact, it was too far from the coastline for me to endure it indefinitely.

I released a deep breath, and Will caressed the back of my fingers with his thumb.

"Feels quite good to be home. This is where we belong, Elle. We'll raise our children here at Eastridge. Not in the city, not in France, but here, where my brothers and I grew up." He lifted my hand and kissed it.

"You know there is nothing that would make me happier."

He smiled, his gaze coming to mine. "And I want nothing more than that."

I watched his blue eyes leave mine and follow the road in front of us. Pretending to search for my little doe as we passed through the north garden, I leaned forward in my seat. But truth be told, I'd adjusted my position to watch Will's irises rouse with white emotion as Eastridge appeared before us.

He loved the place.

And God, I loved him.

He was conquering his fear of fatherhood to give me what he'd promised and to give his children the unconditional love that he had never experienced with his own father.

Will was frightened. I could feel it in his soul and see it in his eyes. A battle raged inside of him. His loving, tender soul warred with the darkness imparted by his upbringing. But he would never be like his father, because unlike Richard Hastings, Will found something he loved more than himself. Richard hadn't counted on that, and it changed the long game. If only Richard could see how his son had changed the game.

Will loved me with desperate abandon.

He had once pleaded for me to hold on to us. *Say the word, Elle,* he had demanded. *Us*. It was one small word, two letters, but it meant everything to him. I'd repeated it back, and he had commanded me to lock down on it, to never let it go. We had learned that our lives were bound by our connection, an obsessive love that had nothing to do with our fathers. Holding that close and keeping it safe was the only way he and I could survive. We both understood that. So we both protected it.

The babies were a tangible extension of what we fiercely defended. Their little bodies were conceived from our bond, and when our babies arrived, we would be able to touch and see and hold in our arms the profound connection that tied us together now and always.

Will would love our children because they were *us*.

He would love all of his children.

I couldn't wait to see him interact with Lissie again. They shared an undeniable connection that had been there from the beginning. She was his princess, and he was her superhero.

The memory of the first time he saw her face came back to me, when she had nailed him hard with her stare. I had wondered then what she'd found in his eyes and what he'd discovered in hers. Now we all know what that was.

"Looks like everyone's home," he said, eyeballing the other cars in the enormous garage as we pulled inside. "I should have dropped you in front of the house, baby. I can pull back round to—"

"No, don't. I'm looking forward to stretching my legs and the fresh air. I'm so glad Thomas could make it home from New York in time. Lissie's birthday is a big deal for our family this year."

He stepped out and rushed to open my door. "How do you think she'll handle the news? About the twins, I mean. We haven't talked about that point."

"Who else knows, Will? Besides your brother, who else knows we're pregnant?" I slipped my hand into his, and we headed for the house. The morning sun warmed my cheeks.

"No one else knows. We'll tell the rest of the family together. We must do it today, Elle. You've changed in the weeks since we were last home, and it won't go unnoticed. We'll tell Mother first. She'll be prepared then, to help explain the logistics to Lissie." He grinned.

I returned the grin and quickly thanked God for my husband and my mother-in-law. "This belly bump came sooner than I expected. Lissie loves Chelsea and caring for the puppies, so I think maybe she'll be excited about the babies. It's time we tell her about her you and Sarah as well."

It was time for Lissie and everyone to know the truth, time to sift through the wreckage as a family and reveal the strong little seedling that would sprout from beneath it all. Lissie was a beautifully spirited little girl who was a joyful breath of fresh air for us all.

"Agreed. If we tell her everything right away, Elle, she'll have an opportunity to ask questions and process it all. I want her to have time with it before her birthday party."

"Let's do it as soon as she gets home from school."

He hesitated.

"You are going to make her happy, Will."

He stopped and pulled me into his arms, and our lips met. We were fixed that way. Our breaths were combined as one, our eyes open—our souls giving and taking the strength between us.

A few hours later, Will and I walked along the shoreline of the English Channel, the northeast wind pushing into our faces, my long hair whipping about us. We settled on the sand in our favorite location beneath Eastridge, where the weather-carved sandstone cliffs provided shelter from the cold wind. I absorbed the energy of the sea and reveled in the sense of harmony it provided. God, it had been so long.

Mary had been thrilled with our news of the pregnancy. After she and my husband were satisfied with the emptiness of my brunch plate, Will had insisted that I have a nap while he spoke to her alone about his first child. I had understood his desire to comfort his mother privately. Learning what Ethan had done with Lissie would hurt Mary.

"This is so perfect," I said, lowering myself onto the quilt between his thighs.

I pressed my back against his chest, and he wrapped me up inside his warm arms. One hand dropped down into my jacket and covered my stomach as if he were protecting our babies. He kissed the top of my head.

"What's inside the bag, Elle?"

"Photos. Beautiful photos of your daughter's first seven years. Shall we have a look?"

Will didn't say a word. His grip on my stomach tightened.

I spun onto my knees to face him and found unshed tears in his eyes.

"You were there with her, baby. The whole time."

"I'll share that with you, Will. I'll show you photos and videos and tell you everything about her."

He nodded, then pulled me to his lips. Our kiss was warm and sweet, as were the words he whispered against my cheek. "I'm deeply grateful for you, Elle. You are everything. You're my flesh and blood savior."

Tears rolled down my cheeks, and his throat tensed as he swallowed his own.

We were different. We had both grown so much. Yet we were exactly the same.

I could feel my home in Will, the place where I had always belonged, and I could feel his broken pieces coming back together again.

I could feel our love for Lissie and for the children growing inside of me.

"I can't wait to feel the babies move for the first time," I whispered against his warm skin.

His blue gaze became a powerful storm of mixed emotions. I gave him a moment to process what was affecting his heart.

My husband pressed his forehead to mine and he smirked.

God, he was so handsome.

I returned the favor with my secret smile.

"No words, baby."

"No words, Will."

Our love was a mutual obsession beyond words. . . .

It was light and dark, joy and pain.

And our beautiful story was one that would never end.

AUTHOR'S NOTE

Dear Reader,

Thanks so much for spending time with my second novel, *Her Lovely Lies*. This one ripped my heart out as I wrote it. I hope the same emotion translates onto the page for you.

If you have a minute, please kindly post a quick review online to help other readers discover it.

Will and Ellie return in *Vows That Bind Us* and again in Thomas's book, *Lies That We Keep*. For more info, visit www.klclare.com.

What happened to Josh Mendes? Turn the page for details!

Don't forget to subscribe to my newsletter for updates at www.klclare.com/newsletter.

Wishing you all the best,

Kelli

GOOD COP BAD BOY

A COCKY HERO CLUB NOVEL

K.L. CLARE

Coming soon from K.L. Clare is a standalone contemporary romance set in Hermosa Beach, California, featuring Josh Mendes from *Lies That Bind Us*.

This novel is part of Vi Keeland and Penelope Ward's Cocky Hero Club, a series of original works inspired by the *New York Times* bestselling Cocky Bastard series.

It will be published by Keeland and Ward in 2020.

Learn more: www.klclare.com

Sign up for the newsletter to receive updates:
www.klclare.com/newsletter

Get alerts for new releases and deals:
www.bookbub.com/authors/k-l-clare

ABOUT THE AUTHOR

Award-winning author K.L. Clare writes contemporary romance and has been praised by industry critics for her elegant prose, captivating and distinctive characters, and original story lines. She lives in Ohio with her two brilliant kids and a sock-thieving spaniel.

If you enjoy Kelli's writing, please follow her on social media or subscribe to her newsletter, where she hosts giveaways along with exclusive writing updates and more.

For behind-the-scenes looks and author chats, join the readers' group: www.facebook.com/groups/klslovelies

www.klclare.com

facebook.com/kellilclare

twitter.com/kellilclare

instagram.com/kellilclare

bookbub.com/authors/k-l-clare

CPSIA information can be obtained
at www.ICGtesting.com
Printed in the USA
FSHW012111290919
62514FS

9 781732 931428